Captivated
by the Cowgirl

Books by Jody Hedlund

Colorado Cowgirls

Committing to the Cowgirl

Cherishing the Cowgirl

Convincing the Cowgirl

Captivated by the Cowgirl

Claiming the Cowgirl: A Novella

Colorado Cowboys

A Cowboy for Keeps

The Heart of a Cowboy

To Tame a Cowboy

Falling for the Cowgirl

The Last Chance Cowboy

Bride Ships Series

A Reluctant Bride

The Runaway Bride

A Bride of Convenience

Almost a Bride

Orphan Train Series

An Awakened Heart: A Novella

With You Always

Together Forever

Searching for You

COLORADO
COWGIRLS
4

Captivated
BY THE Cowgirl

JODY HEDLUND

NORTHERN LIGHTS PRESS

Captivated by the Cowgirl

Northern Lights Press

© 2023 by Jody Hedlund

Jody Hedlund Print Edition

ISBN: 979-8-9852649-9-9

Jody Hedlund www.jodyhedlund.com

Scripture quotations are taken from the King James Version of the Bible.

This is a work of historical reconstruction; the appearances of certain historical figures are accordingly inevitable. All other characters are products of the author's imagination. Any resemblance to actual events or locales or persons, living or dead, is entirely coincidental.

Cover Design by Roseanna White Designs

Cover images from Shutterstock

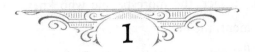

1

Fairplay, Colorado
October 1878

"I would like to hire help." Felicity Courtney tapped on the advertisement she'd carefully crafted before sliding it across the counter toward the store proprietor.

Stoop-shouldered and arthritic, Captain Jim picked up the sheet and held it out as far as his arms could stretch, peering down his nose and attempting to read the print.

"Hire help?" The older man practically shouted the question, his hearing as diminished as his eyesight.

Throughout Simpkins General Store, the other customers halted their browsing of wares. The two fellows sitting on stools on either side of a barrel topped with a checkerboard paused in their game.

Irritation prickled Felicity. Why did she have to live in a small town where people knew everything about everyone? She wanted to glare around and tell folks to mind their own business, but she stifled the urge. The truth was, she needed everyone to know she was looking for help. In fact, the more people who knew about her advertisement, the better.

She flattened her skirt—a fancy emerald color that made her red hair and brown eyes stand out—then she leaned in and read her own handwriting. "Needed: A man who can come out to the homestead once a day to tend to the livestock, chop wood, haul water, and other labor as needed. Wages: One dollar a day."

With a whistle of surprise, Captain Jim handed the sheet back to her. "That there's some good money."

One dollar a day was above the going rate. But both Charity and Patience had insisted she offer at least that amount. No doubt her older sisters felt guilty that she'd been left bearing all the responsibilities of their homestead and boardinghouse by herself while they enjoyed marital bliss with the loves of their lives.

Regardless, the gold mine they'd inherited from their uncle was producing well, and they could afford to pay a generous wage. The money wasn't the issue. The issue was that Felicity hadn't wanted to hire anyone. Had wanted to prove she could get along fine without her sisters.

But after Patience had visited three days ago and found her unconscious on the kitchen floor, Felicity hadn't been able to say no to a plan to hire help, especially after Doctor Steele had examined her and attributed the episode to exhaustion.

Captain Jim whistled again. "I'd offer to do it myself if I wasn't so busy here at the store."

Underneath her chin, she tightened the wide velvet ribbon of her bonnet—which was more of a petite hat set upon the mounds of her fashionably coiled hair. "Thank you, Mr. Simpkins. You're very kind to say so."

A man several feet down the counter, reading a newspaper, gave a soft snort. A snort that belonged to only one person: the annoying Philip Berg.

He was leaning against the counter on both elbows, the sheet of newsprint spread out in front of him. His wavy blond hair hung rakishly over his forehead, as it normally did. And his profile was as cocky and handsome as always. Not that she cared how cocky and handsome he was. It was simply a fact that any living creature would acknowledge.

He was browsing an article, a smirk on his lips. Was he reading something that was causing his mirth? Or did he find her predicament humorous?

He tilted his head, giving her full view of his lean features, sharp and perfectly proportioned—slender nose, prominent chin covered in scruff, and well-defined cheekbones. All chiseled out of smooth mountain granite.

His eyes, the color of a hot spring mirroring a blue

morning sky, locked with hers. He held her gaze as if he could see straight inside her. Then he winked and dropped his attention back to the article in front of him.

Ugh. How dare he wink at her like she was his little sister. Or a giggly girl who was enthralled with him. She hated when he did that, as though he assumed she was ready to throw herself at him at the least bit of attention he gave her.

She'd tried to make it quite clear over the past month of knowing him that she had no interest in him. But he clearly hadn't gotten the message. More likely, he was ignoring it.

Even though he was no longer watching her, she tossed a glare at him anyway. Her situation was no winking matter. It was actually quite serious. Via telegrams, Charity had given her only one week to find help. If she didn't hire someone by the week's end, Charity intended to close up the boardinghouse for the winter and move Felicity into town.

Felicity wasn't necessarily attached to their homestead, and she'd move if necessary. But she'd already rented two rooms to the Kellers, and the older couple had no place else to go. Not with how ill Mr. Keller was.

Of course, her sisters hadn't been pleased to hear about the new boarders. Even though they'd operated the Courtney Boardinghouse for the past year and had rented rooms to plenty of people, Charity and Patience hadn't wanted her taking in anyone because of all the responsibilities that entailed. In fact, they'd told her not to have boarders until Charity and Hudson returned in the spring and instituted their plans to provide a safe residence for poor, homeless women.

However, when Mrs. Keller had arrived with her sick husband in the back of a wagon a couple of weeks ago, Felicity hadn't been able to turn them away. And now, after getting to know them, she couldn't fathom closing up the boardinghouse, not when the Kellers so desperately needed her help.

"Yes, indeed." Felicity spoke again, this time so that hopefully everyone in the store could hear her. "I expect I'll need someone to do a couple of hours of work per day. Likely not much more than that."

She could handle everything else for herself. In fact, the exhaustion of the past week had happened because she hadn't been sleeping well, not because the workload was too much.

But no amount of arguing with Charity or Patience had convinced them otherwise.

Now here she was—attempting to hire help.

She moved away from the counter and let her gaze sweep over the various people still watching her. "If you know of anyone who might be interested, please have them visit me at the boardinghouse to discuss the matter further."

"*Anyone* isn't very specific." Philip's comment was casual and contained a hint of his foreign accent. She didn't know much about where he was from. He hadn't spoken about home or his family during the dinners they'd shared together at Mrs. Bancroft's last month, when she'd been working as the wealthy woman's companion. In fact, Philip's English was so good that she sometimes forgot he was a foreigner.

He read his newspaper a moment longer before glancing up. "I guess that means I can apply for the position."

"I'm only choosing men. Not children."

His grin kicked up on one side, making him too good-looking. Again, she was only stating the obvious—common knowledge accepted far and near.

She knew she ought to feel ashamed of herself for saying such rude things to Philip, but she couldn't seem to help herself—hadn't been able to since the moment she'd met him.

"Maybe you should consider me anyway." His lopsided grin was almost irresistible.

Thankfully, she'd become proficient at not letting it affect her. "I can't, Mr. Berg. I really do need someone who is actually interested in working."

His grin rose higher. "Yes, I can see how that would be a problem, then."

She could feel a smile of her own fighting for release,

and she shifted so that he wouldn't be able to see it. "Good day, Mr. Berg. I wish you much luck finding employment where all you're required to do is play."

"I do like to play." He pushed up from the counter until he was standing at least a head taller than her petite frame. His black coat stretched across his shoulders, hugging his upper body way too closely. "But it's much more pleasurable when I have someone to join in my escapades." His voice dropped low and took on the rumbly quality that never failed to suck the air from the room and make it harder for her to breathe.

No. She dragged in a breath and tried not to let it quiver. Philip Berg was arrogant, impulsive, spoiled, a womanizer . . . She had to keep adding to the list of all the things she didn't like about him to prevent herself from giving in to his charm.

She forced her feet to start across the room, tossing him a parting comment. "Check with the circus. You might find some monkeys willing to play with you."

His laughter burst out, loud and boisterous.

She resisted the urge to turn around and watch him. She knew that with his head thrown back and his face alight with humor, his appeal would be too strong to ignore.

Only after she stepped outside into the chilly October morning did she let her smile break free, and then only briefly. She gathered her cloak tighter as she stopped at the billboard beside the door, where people posted community events and advertisements like hers. Carefully, she extracted two pins from her reticule and began to tack up her help-wanted notice.

She also planned to visit several other stores and hotels to ensure that the word spread. Surely there was a nice fellow, perhaps a miner, who had a little bit of time that he could devote to assisting her every day.

"Felicity," called a man's voice from down the boardwalk behind her.

She didn't have to turn to know who it was. Weston Oakley. He was the latest in a string of suitors who'd pursued her since she and her sisters had moved to Fairplay the previous year. Weston had been trying to convince her to marry him all autumn, especially when she and Patience had almost lost the homestead.

She'd tried to dissuade him. But he hadn't stopped asking.

She ought to give him some credit for his persistence, and yet she didn't want to encourage him. If only she could be as rude to him and make the same cutting comments that she did with Philip. But Weston was too nice for that.

Instead, she fidgeted with the pins in the advertisement, even as the wind fluttered the paper and threatened to wrest it loose. Though the day was sunny, a hint of winter was most definitely in the air.

She cast a glance to the mountain peaks to the west of Fairplay. None of the rocky tops had snow yet. Neither did the range that ran along the other side of the South Park basin to the east. But it wouldn't be long before a dusting covered the mountains with the first pristine layer. The snow would make the passes difficult to traverse and would eventually trap them in the high country until spring.

Perhaps *trap* was a harsh way to describe the feeling that had come over Felicity last winter—one that she was dreading again. But she didn't like the idea that she was stuck in Fairplay. She didn't want to be stuck anywhere.

"Blast it all, Felicity." Weston had stopped beside her, pushed up the brim of his black Stetson, and was staring at the advertisement with all the handsomeness a woman could ever ask for, with his strong features and dark hair and eyes.

She moved the pin again, but the wind flapped at the opposite corner of the advertisement.

"If you needed help, you should've just told me." Weston towered above her, all brawn and muscles not only from ranching his small spread to the north of town but also because of the heavy lifting he did at his mills. With the length of the South Platte River running through his land, he'd done well for himself by building a water-generated sawmill and gristmill. His profits had allowed him to buy up land around town and develop it by constructing both homes and businesses.

For a man of not more than twenty-seven years of age, he'd done well for himself over the past eight years of living in Fairplay. The only thing he hadn't accomplished was finding himself a wife. And not for want of effort. The poor fellow had tried the matrimonial catalogs and had placed advertisements in newspapers with the hope of getting a wife. But none of his relationships had blossomed into marriage.

And now he had his heart set on her.

She stared straight ahead, unable to meet Weston's gaze and the hurt sure to be in his eyes. "You're so busy, Weston. I didn't want to trouble you." Her excuse was only part of the truth.

"I ain't never too busy for you, sweetheart."

The other truth was that she didn't want to let him do anything for her that might make her feel obligated to marry him. "I'm hiring someone for a couple hours a day. That's all."

"Whoa, now. You've got to be careful and can't be hiring any lone dog. No telling if it'll bite."

At just that moment—of course—Philip sauntered outside, tugging his bowler over his unruly blond locks. At the sight of Weston standing beside her, he stopped and his brows rose. "Miss Courtney, I didn't realize you were hiring a dog. If so, then I'm afraid I'm most definitely off your list of possibilities."

"Are you sure about that?" The words were out before she could stop them.

Philip shrugged nonchalantly, but his eyes were alight again. "I do share many similarities to a dog. I am loyal and loving and friendly. I enjoy lots of affection, especially giving kisses."

Kisses? Was he insinuating that he wanted to kiss her? He couldn't be.

His attention flitted to her mouth and then away.

Oh, he most certainly was. Her stomach took a jump off a cliff, falling in a dizzying spin, a sensation she didn't understand or want to feel.

When his grin kicked up, as though he knew exactly his effect upon her, she braced her shoulders. "From what I remember, dog kisses are slobbery and smelly."

Weston's gaze shot back and forth between her and Philip, his brows furrowing as they always did whenever she interacted with Philip. Weston was too kind and straightforward to delve into the word games she played with Philip. But he'd remarked in private that he didn't trust Philip and didn't like it when she talked to him.

Fortunately for Weston, she didn't like talking with Philip either and tried to keep the conversations to rare occasions.

"Are you hiring this fella?" Weston started to reach for her hand, likely to slip it into the crook of his arm as he'd done in the past.

But today, with Philip watching her, she edged past Weston so that she was facing both men. Both made imposing figures—one dark-haired and tough, the other fair-haired and refined. "I don't need you to question my hiring practices."

"Then you are hiring him?" Weston's jaw hardened.

"Yes, I do believe she is." Philip's jaw seemed to flex too, and he held Weston's gaze in a bold, almost authoritative manner, one that proved Philip had a much stronger temperament than he allowed people to see.

"I'll go over each day to help her," Weston insisted.

"She doesn't want your help."

"And she wants yours?"

"Yes."

"No." Felicity had to salvage the situation before the two men started a fistfight. While the attention from men had been flattering when she'd first moved to Fairplay, now at times, it felt stifling.

With the lack of single women in the high country, she knew the best way to stop all the unwanted ardor was to accept Weston's proposal. If she got married, then she'd no longer be sought after. And nineteen years old wasn't too young for marriage. Plenty of women were wedded by her age.

So why couldn't she just accept Weston's proposal? Even though he'd recently built a nice home on his land, he'd offered to come live at the homestead with her after they got married so that she could continue to open the home to those in need. He'd told her he didn't care where they lived as long as they were together—said he wouldn't mind riding out to his property every day for work.

A wavering dizziness clouded her mind, and she pressed a gloved hand against her forehead to keep her balance. "Thank you for your concern, Weston. But I need you to trust me that I'll be careful about who I hire."

He opened his mouth as though he wanted to protest. Then he clamped his jaw shut.

She waited for Philip to make another comment, to say something sarcastic or to jest. But he remained silent too.

With a nod at them both, she turned and strode down the boardwalk.

The truth was, she wasn't ready to settle down. She wanted the freedom to experience life, have adventures, and see more of the world. For a simple woman like her, that was nearly an impossible dream. But she wasn't ready to give it up yet. Especially not for a man.

2

Philip couldn't stop himself from watching Felicity Courtney stride away. With the way her hips swayed and with how the bustle highlighted her backside, his muscles tightened with the need to wrap his hand around her tiny waist and pull her close. She was a fine, fine woman.

But such a fine, fine woman was off-limits to him. Entirely and completely.

"I ain't a fool." Weston Oakley hadn't moved from beside him on the boardwalk. "I can tell you got a big hankering for Felicity."

Hankering? Philip fumbled to translate the meaning of such a word into his native tongue, but he couldn't decipher it. Even so, he could read jealousy in every language. And it was clear Weston coveted Felicity all for himself and didn't want anyone else to pay her any heed.

A sarcastic rebuttal easily formed, one in which he reminded Weston that Felicity had a sharp mind of her own and could easily pick the better man. But Philip bit back his words, something he'd learned to do often over the past months of running and hiding in America.

Ahead, Felicity entered another establishment and disappeared from sight. His last look at her. Ever.

"Just stay away from her." Weston's words echoed with a menacing growl. "Do y'hear?"

Philip rubbed his jaw, the thick layer of stubble so different than his usual clean-shaven style. But then again, so many things about his life were different now. Maybe always would be. Or at least until Gustaf decided to stop hunting him down and trying to assassinate him.

As much as he'd enjoyed sparring with Felicity during his weeks living in South Park, he had no business doing so. He'd chastised himself at least a dozen times to cease such flirtations. But there was something about her—her feistiness, her forthright manner, her quick wit—that he liked immensely. And he hadn't been able to keep from admiring her, the same way he hadn't been able to stop himself from watching her just now.

Weston rested both hands on the handles of his revolvers, holstered in his gun belt. Even if Weston acted tough, Philip was a good judge of character and knew the fellow wouldn't harm a bedbug if he could help it.

"I'm aiming to marry Felicity." Weston spoke as if the deed were almost done.

"I do believe you shall accomplish it." Philip glanced

at his bags packed and sitting outside the livery, awaiting the stagecoach. Declan's bags were piled next to his, and the young man stood a few feet away from the luggage, speaking with the livery owner.

Weston was studying the bags now too, his brows rising. "You leaving town?"

"Yes." Philip's gaze lingered on his camera box and the tripod beside it. He'd photographed many places in and around Fairplay and South Park in an effort to document his travels. But an unfinished feeling nagged him. What had he missed?

Weston cleared his throat. "Well, reckon I oughta let you get to it."

Philip allowed himself to meet Weston's gaze. "Take good care of her. She's a treasure." A treasure? Where had that thought come from? And why had he spoken it aloud?

"I will." Weston touched the brim of his hat in farewell and then strode away, dismissing him and forgetting about him all in one move.

And that's exactly what he wanted, wasn't it? For people to dismiss and forget about him? It was the safest course of action for him and for everyone he met.

His spine prickled with that familiar feeling he was being followed and watched. He surveyed Main Street with the many businesses that lined both sides. Their false fronts made them appear larger than they really were, a common practice in most of the small Western towns he'd visited.

At midday, a few older men loitered about. Several women had congregated outside a shop. Their children were likely in school, a newer brick building one street over. And most men were at their places of employment.

As far as Philip could tell, no one was specifically paying him any attention—not even Weston, especially now that he'd clarified that he had no designs on Felicity.

He narrowed his gaze on the hotel across the street and studied the windows of the second-floor rooms. Just because he couldn't see anyone threatening, it didn't mean an assassin hadn't caught up to him. Gustaf would have hired only the best to track him down and eliminate him.

Which was why he had to leave the South Park valley. After six weeks of being here, he'd already overstayed. Even if he had moved locations from Healing Springs Inn, southwest of town, to Hotel Windsor in Fairplay, he'd still been in the area too long.

Over the past year, he and Declan had usually only stayed a few weeks, maybe a month if they'd really enjoyed the location. Apparently, they'd liked South Park the best. And of course, there was the tiny fact that he liked Felicity Courtney.

Yes, he'd liked her from the first moment he'd sat across from her at one of Mrs. Bancroft's parties. But he'd also known since the outset of his travels that he had to stay clear of female companionship, that his situation was too precarious to involve anyone. Even Declan had agreed they shouldn't spend extended time with any one woman who might later be able to identify Philip.

Thus, they'd kept their dalliances short. Or at least, they'd tried to . . .

Expelling a taut breath, he stepped off the boardwalk and started across the dusty street toward the livery. "When is the stagecoach departing?"

Declan nodded at the livery owner before turning back toward their baggage. "An hour. Long enough to get a last meal at the Hotel Windsor and one more of those delicious hand pies." With his dashing, boyish aura, Declan looked more like he was eighteen instead of twenty-four. His fair hair was similar to Philip's, but he had a rounder face and deeper-set eyes.

They'd met at Cambridge, and Declan had easily become one of his best friends. The fun-loving American had gone home with him the summer after their graduation and had been there when Philip's entire world had crashed down.

At the time, Gustaf had been king of Lapland for approximately a year after their father's passing, and Philip hadn't been aware of the trouble his older brother had been causing. But it hadn't taken long after his return to Lapland to discover Gustaf had dissolved the modern bicameral parliament that their father had established. Not only had he disbanded parliament, but he'd dismissed the prime minister as well as the cabinet.

Gustaf had also begun imprisoning his political opponents and any dissidents to his regime. Worst of all, he'd locked up a group of poor rebels who'd protested his callous disregard of their fishing rights, and he'd hanged several to make an example of them.

Numerous politicians, including the prime minister, had approached Philip about taking the throne in Gustaf's place. No one had said they were planning a coup to overthrow Gustaf, but it was clear that people were dissatisfied with Gustaf's heavy-handed methods and his disregard for the government. His wasteful spending and attempts at raising taxes had made him even more unpopular.

Philip had been home less than a month when Gustaf had learned of the secretive meetings taking place to oust him and make Philip king. And Gustaf's reaction had been less than pleased. He'd hired an assassin to attack and kill Philip in his bedchamber.

And that's when the prime minister and other officials had advised Philip to go into hiding, at least until the rebellion had the chance to gain more ground and support. Once the rebels found a way to overthrow Gustaf, the leading government officials planned to call Philip home as the next king of Lapland. But of course,

Gustaf didn't want that to happen and had continued his efforts to remove the threat Philip posed.

"What do you say?" Declan waggled his eyebrows. "One last meal?"

"Certainly. Why not." Philip had grown weary of American fare almost from the start of his journey. But Declan had an easy way about him that had made him the perfect traveling companion, always willing to try new things, be independent, and live simply.

Declan was well aware of the danger involved in traveling with Philip. But his friend had insisted on accompanying him anyway, helping him navigate through America and proving to be a lively and interesting companion.

Only this morning, Declan had realized he'd run out of funds. Coming from a well-to-do Eastern family with several homes and many servants, he'd telegrammed his parents, who were more than willing to continue to supply the necessary money for his traveling. But they'd sent the money to a bank in Denver rather than Fairplay, just in case anyone was surveying Declan and his family for ties to Philip.

Now, with the need to go to the bank in Denver, they really had no more reason to delay their departure from Fairplay.

Whenever Philip ran low on funds, he didn't need to say anything. An envelope addressed to him with more cash always showed up at his residence. It was uncanny. But he accepted the money gratefully.

With a happy whistle, Declan started across the street toward Hotel Windsor, and Philip fell into step beside him. As nonchalantly as possible, he searched for any sign that someone was spying on him. But the spine-tingling feeling of being watched was gone. If anyone had been there, they no longer were.

Not for the first time since he'd fled from his country, the doubts rose to taunt him. Had he done the right thing in siding with parliament and the prime minister? Should he have supported his brother instead? Could he have worked to influence Gustaf to do better and be a fairer king, as their father had been before them?

Declan opened the door of the hotel and held it for Philip. Even though Philip had urged Declan not to show him preferential treatment, Declan hadn't been able to toss aside the manners and formalities entirely.

Philip breathed in the waft of chicken stew—a common meal at the hotel—and started through only to find himself face-to-face with Felicity Courtney. Again.

He hadn't anticipated seeing her in Simpkins General Store earlier—had gone in to read the newspaper that came up from Denver, always searching for news about his country and his brother. But as usual, there hadn't been anything.

He actually hadn't seen Felicity as often as he would

have liked over the past three weeks since she'd left Mrs. Bancroft's and returned to her home—only occasionally around town and at church. One time he'd purposefully set up his camera on the road leading to her home so that he'd be able to encounter her. Okay, maybe he'd done it twice.

But this second meeting in a day was more than he could have hoped for.

Not that he'd been hoping to see her again. But he wouldn't complain about having another chance to take in her stunning features, so delicate and yet so strong at the same time. Her skin was creamy, contrasting her rich auburn hair. And her eyes . . . the brown was as luxurious as the softest and warmest sable.

He could admit that she was the most beautiful woman he'd ever laid eyes on. Since he was leaving so soon, there was no harm in acknowledging such a thing now, was there?

"Miss Courtney." He eyed her with a quirked brow. "If you want to hire me, you could just ask me instead of manufacturing all of these accidental meetings."

She released a low scoffing sound, one that never failed to rub against him and stir the insatiable need to banter with her. "Why, Mr. Berg. I didn't realize you were so desperate for work that you had to follow me around." She fisted a hand on her waist, outlining the gentle curve of her hip and length of her thigh.

If he were a mutt, his tongue would be hanging out and he'd be panting for her. No, he wasn't ashamed to admit it. She was every man's dream. And it was no wonder that Weston Oakley and most of the single male population of Colorado drooled over her.

The problem was that Weston couldn't handle Felicity's sharp mind and spunk. She needed someone who could dole out the boldness in the same measure while also being able to temper her spirit without destroying it.

The dozen or so round tables were filled with customers—mostly men—taking their noon meal. The hum of voices was low, so that the clank of silverware against porcelain rang out. All eyes seemed to be upon Felicity. And him.

Their sparring was no secret.

Others seemed to find as much entertainment in watching them as Philip did in riling her up. "Just admit it, Miss Courtney. All along you've been looking for a way to get me out to your boardinghouse so you can have me all to yourself."

A lovely shade of pink infused her cheeks at his insinuation. And although he never crossed the line into impropriety, he guessed this time he was toeing it a little too closely.

She lifted her chin, and her eyes flashed with a spark he relished seeing there. "Mr. Berg, if I need a doormat, have no fear, I'll call upon you to provide your services."

How did she always have such witty replies? He loved it and couldn't hold back his smile of appreciation.

She pressed her pretty lips together in self-satisfaction. Then she took a step to pass by him. Except that she wobbled, and her hand fluttered to her temple. At the same time, she closed her eyes but wavered again.

Something was wrong. Suddenly all mirth fled from him, and he reached out to steady her. When she didn't resist, unease shot through him.

As she opened her eyes and glanced up at him, her expression filled with vulnerability. "I don't know what's wrong with me. I'm so dizzy. And tired."

Before he could respond, her eyes rolled back, and she began to collapse.

His reflexes were quick, and he managed to scoop her up so that he was cradling her against his chest. "Felicity?" he called to her gently, urgently.

Around him, men had jumped up from their tables, their faces mirroring the surprise and concern he felt.

Beside him, Declan was already opening the hotel door. "We should take her to the doctor's office. The sign in the window says the doctor's in."

"Quite right. The doctor. That's what she needs." Philip hurried outside, carrying her as carefully as he could.

Her head lolled against his shoulder and then tipped

back, revealing her pale face and dark circles under her eyes.

What was wrong with her?

With a knot tightening his stomach, he strode down the street toward the small, weathered building with a white sign above the door that said *Doctor's Office*. Another sign, this one painted brightly, hung in the window and had the names of the two doctors: *Dr. Astrid Steele and Dr. Logan Steele.*

Philip found it somewhat unusual that a town as sparsely populated as Fairplay had two doctors, including a female physician. But he wasn't opposed to women becoming educated and using their God-given talents the same as men. In fact, he'd approved his father's efforts to open universities to women.

Felicity stirred in Philip's arms, her lashes rising. "I'm fine," she whispered. "Just tired. That's all."

Fine? Just tired? Philip couldn't keep a snort from escaping.

"Last time this happened, I was back on my feet in no time."

He halted in front of the door. "Last time?"

She nodded almost wearily, then closed her eyes again. "I just need to get more sleep."

"How many people have you known to pass out when they're tired?"

"Hmmm . . ." Her soft thinking sound drew his

attention to her mouth, to her gently rounded lips, to her smooth cheeks, to the elegant curve of her chin and jaw . . .

What was he doing? He couldn't get distracted by the feel of her body in his arms or the way she smelled faintly of strawberries and cream. "Or maybe there's another condition you're suffering from that needs further investigating."

Her eyes flew open, suddenly wide and filled with worry. "Do you think so?"

"Yes."

She held his gaze, likely needing to know he was serious and not teasing this time. He kept his expression grave. As he carried her through the door and into the empty waiting room, she didn't protest.

A tall, distinguished doctor guided him into an office. As Philip gently placed Felicity on the examining table, he debated offering to stay by her side. He wanted to hear what the doctor had to say about her condition and why she was fainting. But he had no ties to Felicity that gave him any right to insist, and so he retreated into the waiting room and took a seat.

Declan lowered himself into the chair beside him.

Philip may have once been too spoiled to consider the needs of his friends, but the trials and hardships of the past year had opened his eyes and taught him much. Philip knew Declan would do anything he asked, even if that meant staying in Fairplay and delaying their move to Denver.

But he didn't want to ask that of Declan. The young man had done so much for him—had followed him each step of the journey, supporting and encouraging him, and hadn't complained once.

Philip sat straight, his backbone stiff. "I don't feel right leaving Felicity in her condition, especially without any help at her boardinghouse."

"Are you planning to stay and help her?"

"Perhaps." He wasn't entirely sure what he intended to do. All he knew was that he couldn't walk away while she was in this condition and in need of help. "Regardless, I want you to go to the hotel and have that last hand pie. Then leave on the stage today."

Declan shook his head. "No, I couldn't—"

"I insist. You've been looking forward to visiting Denver, and you'll get the replenishment of funds you've been needing."

"I don't mind waiting for you."

"I'll tarry here another day or two, make sure Felicity is situated, and then I'll head down to Denver and meet up with you."

Declan studied his face as though trying to read his emotions, but Philip had learned long ago how to keep his feelings concealed and put up his best front.

"You're sure?" Declan glanced around the waiting

room and then to the street, making sure no one was privy to their conversation.

"A couple more days won't hurt me." At least, he prayed it wouldn't.

Besides, Felicity wouldn't want him around once she was feeling better. For now, however, while she was weak, he could accompany her back to her boardinghouse and then ride into town to personally hire a fellow to give her a hand with the workload. If he had to, he'd go door to door until he found someone.

He had to assist her in the matter because doing so was decent and right. Not because she was special to him.

Declan dropped his voice. "It's been obvious you like her since the day you met her, but—"

"Obvious?" Philip released a scoffing laugh that came out too loud. "No, that's not true."

"Oh, come on. Your attraction to her has wound so tight I've just been waiting for it to snap."

"We can't be around each other without sparring."

"Sparring with plenty of sparks."

"I've engaged in a little harmless flirtation. That's all."

Declan clamped a hand on Philip's shoulder. "Deny it all you want, but that won't make it go away."

Philip couldn't deny he found Felicity attractive. But he had no intentions toward her. None. He wouldn't allow himself to consider any woman now. Not when he was in so much danger and on the run for his life.

Even if he hadn't been in such danger, he was a prince with royal obligations and didn't have the option to pursue a woman of his own choosing. Lapland law stipulated that royal matches had to be made and approved by a majority of members of parliament. Gustaf's wife had been carefully selected by a committee tasked with the purpose of finding a bride. And the committee had started the process of looking for a wife for Philip. While they would consult him over their final choices, Philip had grown up knowing what would be expected of him and hadn't questioned it.

Yes, he liked Felicity. The attraction was *tight*. Declan wasn't wrong on either score. But Philip had kept his feelings for her under control, had done his best to hold her at arm's length. For her safety. And because he didn't want to lead her on only to break her heart.

He'd had one such relationship while at Cambridge, and in the end, when he'd had to sever the ties, the parting of ways had been so hurtful and difficult he'd vowed not to give a woman false hope ever again.

"Nothing has developed between Felicity and myself over the past weeks." He spoke earnestly, needing to reassure himself as much as Declan. "And nothing will happen in a couple of days."

"I'm sure you're right." Declan stood, a knowing glint in his eyes.

Philip rose too. "I'll make sure she's taken care of and

then be on my way."

Grinning, Declan started toward the door.

"I'll be on the first stage out tomorrow morning."

"Sure you will." Declan opened the door and stepped out.

"You'll see."

His friend gave a mock salute before disappearing outside.

Unsettled, Philip lowered himself back into the chair. The logical, rational part of his brain told him to rush after Declan and leave today.

But with a glance toward the closed door of the examining room, his heartbeat stuttered a protest. If he was perfectly honest with himself, he had to admit he'd already had a difficult time tearing himself away from Felicity and Fairplay when she'd been doing well and managing fine. He'd kept delaying, kept telling himself he needed a few more photos. If not for Declan's dwindling finances, he might have stayed longer.

How could he possibly leave her now that she wasn't doing well or managing fine? There was no way. Not until he was certain she would be well looked after during his absence.

His absence? As if his going away would only be temporary. As if he intended to someday return. He almost snorted at the notion. Once he left Fairplay, he'd never be back, and he'd never see Felicity Courtney again.

He couldn't pretend otherwise.

With a mental shake, he forced himself to replay the litany of advice he'd been giving himself all along: Felicity was simply a pretty distraction, one that had helped to take his mind off his troubles for a short while. But that's all she was. A fleeting encounter.

He would depart—soon—and that was all there was to it.

3

"I can walk just fine now, Mr. Berg." Felicity squirmed against Philip as he carried her from the wagon to her house. But the moment she moved, she was all too aware of the hard wall of his body shielding her, the muscular arms holding her up underneath her backside, and the closeness of his chin near her cheek and forehead.

"The physician said you are to stay off your feet today." His words were as firm now as they'd been in town when he'd carried her to the wagon and helped her onto the bench.

"Dr. Steele's advice is just that. Advice." Felicity didn't want to admit to how tired and dizzy she still was for fear that Philip would go and tell Patience. If Patience found out about another spell, she'd insist on Felicity moving over to the Trout Creek Ranch with her. Or she'd come and stay with Felicity, sacrificing being with her new husband and daughter.

Philip started up the front steps. "Advice is meant to be followed."

"Only if you agree with the advice. Which I do not."

"I do. You need to rest today and sleep well tonight."

"I have too much to do to sit around." Someone had to take care of the livestock and provide a meal and draw water for the Kellers. And someone had to do the cleaning and laundry and the hundred and one other daily chores. There were still a few last root vegetables that needed to be harvested and stored in the cellar. And more firewood to be chopped in preparation for the winter.

Philip crossed the front porch and somehow managed to open the door and enter without disturbing her in the least. Once inside, he paused and took in the room. Felicity knew she had nothing for which to be embarrassed. She kept the place immaculate. Even so, Philip and Declan were wealthier than she was, probably from a different social class altogether. And though her home was well furnished, nothing was fancy or opulent. The place was actually quite simple and decorated with all of Patience's many creations.

He started toward a grouping of furniture on one side of the front room, opposite the long dining room table. As he stopped beside the sofa, he hesitated.

She was too mortified by the whole affair to look at his face or into his eyes, unwilling to see the humor that might be lurking there. Even though he'd been serious all throughout the doctor's visit and the ride back to the boardinghouse, she guessed it was only a matter of time before he found something to tease her about.

"If I deposit you onto the sofa, you must promise to stay there until your help arrives."

"And if I don't promise you?"

"Then I shall sit with you and make sure you do."

"I doubt you have the patience to play nursemaid to me."

"Test me." His voice dropped low by her ear. "I dare you."

Her stomach did a series of strange flips. If there was one thing she'd learned about Philip Berg, it was that he was adventurous and afraid of very little. Including her.

"Very well." She would simply pretend to rest until he left. Besides, hired help wouldn't be arriving—at least, not that she anticipated, since she'd had no solid inquiries regarding her advertisement.

Philip started to lower her but then halted. "I can tell you're only saying what you think I want to hear. But that strategy won't work with me."

She expelled an exasperated breath. "Put me down, Philip." The moment she spoke his Christian name, she mentally slapped herself at the informality. Hopefully, he wouldn't pick up on it.

His lips quirked into a smirk. "So we are finally calling each other by our given names, Felicity?"

Of course he wouldn't let the mistake pass him by. Of course he would make a big deal out of it, especially since she'd insisted on calling him by his proper name even after he'd given her leave to use his first name instead after one of their first dinners.

"Put me down, *Mr. Berg*."

"Too late. You already called me Philip, and you cannot take it back."

"I am taking it back."

He didn't move but held her poised above the sofa. His breath was warm against her cheek and ear. "Felicity. Felicity. Felicity."

His words brushed gently across her skin, and each mention of her name—especially with the slight accent that dragged her name out on his tongue—flipped her stomach end over end.

"You must call me Miss Courtney." Her voice lacked power and conviction. Because she was tired, not because she was falling under his spell.

He finally lowered her to the sofa, placing her on the cushions with as much care as though she were a breakable crystal vase. As he released her, he reached for the quilted blanket on the back of the sofa and began to drape it over her.

She knew she ought to protest such tender ministrations. But as his eyes cut to her, they also seemed to cut right through her, slicing her open, so that every last drop of air escaped, and she had no way to form the words of objection.

He tucked the edges of the quilt around her before straightening and peering down at her, his eyes a shade of blue that was too mesmerizing. The errant blond strand fell across his forehead—the strand that always begged for combing back. His jaw flexed, drawing her attention to the chiseled shape and the scruffiness of his stubble.

Ugh. He really was too good-looking, especially standing above her in her house and looking at her with concern.

She tried to frown at him. "Don't be so nice to me."

His brows rose. "Has it become a crime to be nice?"

"I like you better when you're not so serious."

"You like me."

A grin worked at the corner of her lips. "Absolutely not."

"You just said so."

There. She breathed easier. They were back on more familiar ground. "I suppose you're here to torment me?"

"Yes, exactly." He bent and tucked the blanket around her tighter. "I'm here to torment you by making sure you stay off your feet."

"Don't you have someplace else you need to be?"

"I've postponed leaving town until tomorrow."

"You're leaving?" Her question tumbled out before she could stop it, her pulse tumbling right along with it.

"Do I detect a note of sadness in your question, *Felicity?*" His eyes suddenly took on a twinkle.

Irritation welled up, mostly at herself for giving him any ammunition to use against her. "There's no sadness, *Mr. Berg.* Only curiosity."

"You're hoping I'll tell you where I'm going so that you can follow after me?"

His response was so ludicrous she could only roll her eyes and scoff.

"Since you insist on knowing, I can tell you I'll be staying in Denver for a few weeks."

She shouldn't have been surprised he was moving on. He and Declan had made it clear all along that they were only in South Park for a short time. They'd come to see the sights, hike the mountains, and experience the high country. Philip was an amateur photographer as well and had been taking pictures every place he visited.

She could admit she envied their ability to travel the country, that they could go wherever they wanted, even this remote little town. Of course Healing Springs Inn, with the hot spring, probably had enticed them to the area. And apparently Declan's family also had a connection to Mrs. Bancroft—something about the older lady being a godparent to one of Declan's parents, which was another reason the two had stopped in South Park.

Whatever the case, Philip had hinted often enough over the past weeks that his life was back in his country, that he had no choice but to return at the end of his travels, that he had obligations and didn't have the freedom to veer off course.

Philip took a tentative step back from the sofa and eyed the door, almost as if he was anxious to escape the house and leave the high country at that very moment.

"Please, don't let me keep you from your next exciting destination." Now that he'd revealed his plans, she finally understood why Declan had been standing in front of the livery next to a stack of bags, including Philip's camera equipment. They'd been readying to leave.

Had Philip planned to say goodbye to her? Or had he intended to leave town without even a distant farewell?

Why did she care at all?

"Declan is going on ahead." Philip stuffed his hands into his pockets, his shoulders suddenly stiff. "But I decided to stay to make sure you got home adequately."

His statement sounded a little bit like an embarrassed confession. She wanted to tease him, knew he'd tease her if their roles were reversed. But for a reason she couldn't explain, his admission filled her with a strange pleasure. He'd put off leaving in order to help her. That was one of the nicest things anyone had ever done for her.

She ought to thank him.

She fidgeted with a loose thread on the blanket covering her, afraid to give voice to the gratitude for fear he'd hear her pleasure.

"Miss Courtney?" The timid call of Mrs. Keller came from the stairwell.

The waif of a woman moved soundlessly in her slippered feet and always seemed to be taking Felicity by surprise. She stood on the middle step, still in her robe at midday. Her gray hair was flattened on one side, and blanket creases lined her cheek.

Felicity didn't blame the woman for sleeping whenever she could, even at midday. She was up at all hours of the day and night caring for her husband and never seemed to get any good length of sleep.

Felicity pushed herself up to her elbows and immediately fought against a dizzy wave. "How is Mr. Keller?"

"He's awake." Mrs. Keller clutched her robe closed, her tired eyes upon Philip warily. "I was coming to get the warm water for his bed bath."

Felicity released a tired groan and tried to sit up, but Philip was at her side in the next instant, gently easing her back down. "No. You're not going anywhere." His voice had that note of authority that came out from time to time. It wasn't bossy. Rather, it was an unquestioning assumption that she would do as he'd declared. The firmness of his tone was matched by the determination in his eyes.

"Is something wrong?" Mrs. Keller's soft voice wavered.

Felicity wanted to stand up and declare that she was perfectly alright. Mrs. Keller had enough to worry about with her husband's care and didn't need the burden of Felicity's health issues upon her too.

Before she could figure out how to answer, Philip was already providing an explanation. "Miss Courtney has fainted twice this week. The physician believes she needs more rest as well as more help here at the boardinghouse."

Still halfway up the stairway, Mrs. Keller shook her head sadly. "This is my fault. I never should have agreed to let you take a shift with my husband each night."

Philip's brows shot up, and his gaze pinned Felicity. "What is the duration of such shifts?"

Felicity glared back, unwilling to let Philip intimidate her. "I'm doing so to give Mrs. Keller time to sleep."

"I realize that. But how long are you awake?"

Mrs. Keller wavered before clutching the rail. "Felicity has been more than gracious to allow me four hours of uninterrupted sleep."

Philip's expression didn't have a trace of humor, was as deadly serious as Felicity had ever seen it. "So exactly how much sleep are you getting?"

She tried to calculate, but she honestly couldn't remember. Her days and nights had become so jumbled that she didn't know anymore. Regardless, she had to get up and fetch water for the Kellers. Mr. Keller had bed sores that needed bathing every day, open wounds that would fester if not taken care of properly.

She swung her legs over the edge of the sofa.

Philip made a dangerous growly sound. Then he lifted her feet off the ground and swung them back on the cushions.

"Philip, stop. I have work that can't wait." Ugh. She'd done it again. Used his given name.

He wrapped the blanket snugly around her legs. Hopefully he was too caught up making her a prisoner inside the quilt and hadn't heard her. "Give me a list of what needs to be done, and I'll do it."

"There's too much."

"I'll be the judge of that."

"I didn't think you liked to work. And even if you did, you probably wouldn't know how to complete the tasks."

He straightened, and the slant of his brows warned her not to move again. "I might surprise you with how much I've learned to do this past year of traveling."

"You will definitely surprise me." Oh, the magnetic pull of those blue eyes. They were like lassos wrapping around her every time, cinching hard and dragging her toward him.

"Good." His voice took on a mirthful ring. "Now give me your list and let me try it."

She sighed, too tired to fight him. "We need at least two buckets of water. The stove needs to be fueled and water set to heat. The horse needs tending. The wood needs chopping. And I should get something simmering for supper soon, perhaps make some bread."

"That sounds easy enough."

"Easy?" She released a half laugh. "Only in your dreams."

"So you're dreaming about me now, are you?" He flashed a smile at her—one that definitely would have her dreaming about him. Not that she'd admit anything of the sort to him.

"I'm dreaming about how I can get you to go away." That wasn't true.

And as his smile widened, it was clear he knew she was bluffing.

Mrs. Keller hadn't moved from her spot on the step and had been watching their interaction with ever-widening eyes. As though recognizing the same, Philip gave her one of his charming smiles. "If you make sure Felicity doesn't get up from the sofa while I'm working, I promise I'll get the water for your husband ready first."

She nodded and glanced at Felicity. "I'll do my best."

"At the very least, you can let me know if she arises from the sofa while I'm outside. Then I can administer my own special form of discipline later."

Special form of discipline? Tingles raced over Felicity's skin. Maybe she'd get up at least once just to see what he had in mind.

As his gaze locked with hers, he seemed to read the rebellion within her, and his eyes lit. "Don't you dare lift a finger from the sofa."

He was taunting her. But she couldn't keep from loving it. She lifted her fingers one at a time and taunted him right back.

With mock sternness, he folded his arms. "Guess you're asking for it, aren't you?"

"I'm actually really scared and trembling in fear of what you'll do to me."

He chuckled and then crossed to the door. With his hand on the knob, he paused and tossed another comment to Mrs. Keller. "Also, keep track of how many times she refers to me as Philip, will you?"

With that, he winked at Felicity and exited the house.

As his footsteps faded, she couldn't stop herself from grinning like a silly old maid. Her body relaxed into the sofa, and her eyelids suddenly felt weighted by boulders. How long had it been since someone had taken care of her? Had helped carry her burdens?

It had been too long.

Now finally, with Philip there, somehow she sensed she was alright, that she wasn't alone anymore. And that was all she needed to know to fall into a deep sleep.

4

Philip brought the wagon to a stop near the barn. From the corner of his eye, he waited for the front door to open and for Felicity to storm out, demanding to know why he'd returned.

The evening was growing dark, and the low glow in a window told him a lantern had been lit. But the boardinghouse was as quiet now as it had been a couple of hours ago when he'd ridden into town.

Was she still asleep? He hoped so.

All afternoon, he'd hauled water, chopped wood, fed the livestock, and tended to other needs around the place. Every time he'd come inside, he'd expected her to be bustling about and order him to leave. But every time, she'd remained asleep on the sofa right where he'd left her.

Finally, when the afternoon had grown late and he'd had no more reason to stay, he'd made a list of items that she needed—feed for the chickens, grain for the horse, kerosene for lanterns, a new bucket for hauling water, and several other essentials he'd noticed were low. He'd told himself he'd ride into town, purchase the things for her, and then do his best to locate the help she needed.

But as he'd stood outside the store and started loading the wagon with all the supplies, his gut had cinched with protest at the thought of approaching any one of the dozens of men now arriving in town after the day spent mining or ranching.

He didn't want to hire a strange fellow to ride out to the boardinghouse and work for Felicity. Instead, he'd rather find someone reputable, reliable, and preferably someone who wouldn't drop down on one knee and propose marriage to Felicity the first time he saw her.

He'd made a few half-hearted inquiries but then had gone to Hotel Windsor and located his bags and belongings in the lobby where Declan had stowed them, likely assuming he'd stay there another night. But instead of taking the bags up to a room, Philip had carried them to the wagon bed and promptly driven back to the boardinghouse.

As he descended from the wagon seat, he watched the house again.

Still no sign of Felicity.

He rounded the wagon and pulled out his camera case and the tripod. What was she going to say when she saw his bags and belongings? Her lush brown eyes would flash, and her pert lips would purse together, then she'd release her fury upon him.

She wouldn't want him there.

It had been one thing for him to deliver her back to her house after her fainting episode. And she'd only protested a little when he'd insisted on helping her so that she could rest.

But she hadn't agreed to letting him stay there for the night. And he doubted she ever would.

So then, what, exactly, was he doing at the boardinghouse instead of taking a room in the hotel?

He still hadn't been able to make sense of his actions. Not even after the quiet mile back. The only thing that came to mind was that he was worried about her and wanted to make sure she got enough sleep overnight.

Whatever she'd been doing to help her boarders had been noble and kind. Mrs. Keller looked frazzled and worn and in desperate need of assistance. But Felicity couldn't miss so much sleep night after night and still function.

That had become obvious. At least to him.

As he lifted out the rest of his bags and set them on the ground, his gaze caught upon the aspen leaves in their gold finery, showcased by the fiery reds and oranges that hovered over the western range, causing the sky to glow and reminding him of the majestic mountains of his homeland.

His heart gave a thud of longing for the land of his birth, the country he loved, and the many people he'd left behind—including his mother, younger sister Estelle, many cousins, and friends. After close to twelve months of being gone, the ache of missing them hadn't gone away. At times it only stung a little. But sometimes—like now—his chest reverberated with the pain of all he'd lost. And it hurt with the reality that his brother—his own flesh and blood—had wanted to murder him.

Although only two years apart in age, he and Gustaf had never been close. They'd been sent to different boarding schools and later to different universities. Even so, they were brothers, and that had to count for something, didn't it?

Of course he could understand Gustaf feeling betrayed, undermined, and rejected by so many countrymen asking for him to resign so that Philip could be king in his stead.

Even so, Philip had never imagined his brother would attempt an assassination.

Assassination.

Philip surveyed the dark corners of the homestead, the hills, and the woodland beyond the house. Was the assassin out there even now, just waiting to strike? He could only hope against hope that Gustaf had given up on trying to kill him.

If only he could simply pack up everything and return

home. He was tired of running and hiding.

The truth was, Philip had never aspired to be king. In fact, while growing up, he'd played his role as the second son well, never offending his older brother, always deferring, always staying in Gustaf's good graces.

He hadn't sought out the conflict, still didn't want it. But his duty to his country swelled within him stronger than his familial bond. His country needed a king who put the people first, who cared about the country's prosperity over his own, who was willing to sacrifice his needs for them. If Gustaf wouldn't aspire to be that kind of king, then he left Philip with no choice but to take his place and do it in his stead.

Whatever the case, he was still here in Fairplay when he should have left for a new hiding place. And now he was at the Courtney Boardinghouse, the last place he ought to be. Not only was he potentially bringing danger to Felicity's doorstep, but he was throwing himself into a tempting situation—a beautiful red-headed temptation.

He expelled a sigh.

Yes, this was the last place he should have come.

He glanced at his stuff, at the wagon bed, then at the house.

He'd stay just one night and take the shift with Mr. Keller so that both Mrs. Keller and Felicity could catch up on their sleep. In the morning, he'd go back to town and find a hired hand for her. This time he'd do it no matter how much he didn't want to. Then he'd leave as he'd planned. He had no other alternative.

With fresh resolve, he tended to the horse and did a few last outside tasks. By the time he'd finished, darkness had completely fallen, and he finally hauled his bags to the house. At the front door, he paused and considered knocking. But at the silence on the other side, he quietly let himself in.

His gaze went immediately to the sofa.

Felicity was still lying where he'd left her. She'd turned to her side, and the covers had come loose and hung down onto the floor, her skirt twisted around her legs. But otherwise, her eyes were closed, and her chest rose and fell in the rhythm of deep sleep.

As he set down his bags, the soft pad of Mrs. Keller's feet resounded on the stairway. Still clutching the same robe, her gray hair as disheveled as earlier, she came halfway down and watched him warily. He supposed she had every right to question why he was there the same way he'd been questioning himself.

"I'll take Felicity's shift with your husband tonight." He spoke as quietly as possible so that he didn't disturb Felicity. Thankfully, she didn't stir.

Mrs. Keller opened her mouth as though to protest, but he spoke first.

"If you'll show me what to do, I'm sure I shall be an adequate substitute." He knew nothing about nursing.

But he'd also known nothing about surviving on his own before he'd run away from home. At the boarding school and university, he'd always had servants and bodyguards to assist him. He'd never had to dress himself, cook a meal, or even saddle his own horse.

During his travels, he'd grown self-sufficient and rather liked the satisfaction of not having to rely on others for everything. He and Declan had stayed in some rustic and humble places—places where he'd had to sleep on the ground, cook or go hungry, chop wood or freeze.

If he could learn all that, he could surely tend to a sick man.

Mrs. Keller's expression held indecision.

"We need to give Felicity a break tonight." He spoke the words firmly, having no trouble insisting on having his way, especially in this regard.

Her shoulders finally fell. "He can't be left alone for more than a few minutes at a time."

He waited for her to explain her husband's condition.

Instead, she nodded toward the door that led into the dark kitchen. "Felicity usually provides warm broth and other liquid food that I can give to him."

His own stomach chose that moment to rumble with hunger. "I'll see what I can find and bring something up."

"I'm not sure if Felicity—"

"Give me a few moments." He didn't wait for her to agree to his plan and instead gathered the lamp and crossed into the kitchen.

It was as tidy and clean as the rest of the house, with a large cast iron stove in one corner, a worktable at the center, a sink near the back door, and shelves and pantry cabinets that seemed well stocked.

After stoking the embers in the stove, he soon had a blaze and began heating a pot, which appeared to contain chicken broth. He rummaged through a cabinet to find canned beans, salt pork, and half a loaf of bread.

While he couldn't cook anything fancy, he was able to manage warming up the few items and putting together a plate for Mrs. Keller along with a bowl of the broth. Mrs. Keller met him at the top of the steps and took the offering gratefully.

When Philip had finished his own simple fare, he set aside a plate in the warmer for Felicity before washing the dishes. As the chill of the late October night began to seep into the house, he added fuel to the stove in the front room and covered Felicity with another blanket before making his way upstairs to the Kellers' room.

The air was warm and musty and had a lingering scent of urine. Mr. Keller lay motionless in the center of the bed. The lantern on the bedside table illuminated ashen skin, a skeletal body, and a nearly bald head, save a few thin tendrils of silver hair.

He was propped up by several pillows, high enough that Mrs. Keller, in the chair beside the bed, could spoon sips of broth between his lips. Even though Mr. Keller's body appeared to be flaccid and useless, his eyes were bright and alive, and as they landed upon Philip, they widened.

"Good evening, Mr. Keller." Philip tipped his head to acknowledge the older man.

He seemed to try to nod in return, but he'd obviously lost most of his bodily functions. From apoplexy or what some doctors referred to as a stroke?

The chest of drawers on the opposite wall was covered with bottles of medicines and herbal remedies. A chamber pot in the corner was overdue for emptying. And a basin of water on the floor also needed dumping. Another smaller bowl on the bedside table held a suction-like item.

Whatever ailed the man, he was clearly ill and in great need of assistance.

"I came to introduce myself." Philip crossed to the bed so that the light shone on him more directly.

At his approach, Mr. Keller took him in, studying Philip's face intensely before dropping to the length of him. When his sights returned to Philip's face a moment later, there was recognition in the man's eyes. And excitement.

Philip took a small step back. This man couldn't possibly know anything about him or his past. No one else had during the months of traveling. Of course, Philip had grown out his hair and left his face covered in perpetual scruff. And he'd attired himself in the simple wool trousers and wool shirts of working men, hoping to blend in.

Mr. Keller stared at him with ever-widening eyes. Then he opened his mouth as though to say something, but only a gurgle came out.

Mrs. Keller paused in scooping up another spoonful of broth and turned her gaze sharply upon Philip. "My husband seems to think he knows you."

Mr. Keller blinked, as if to agree with his wife's pronouncement. The man might not be able to move or talk, but his mind was apparently still strong. As was his eyesight. Even so, surely the fellow didn't know he was Prince Carl Philip Glucksberg of the small Scandinavian nation of Lapland.

"I'm sorry, sir. But you're likely mistaking me for someone else."

Mr. Keller's eyes didn't move from Philip's face. Instead, they remained fixed there, a sense of awe and wonder and even respect shining in ever-growing intensity.

Perhaps the man had once seen his father. Philip did resemble his father in appearance. In fact, his father's portrait from his youth was nearly identical to Philip's.

Mrs. Keller watched her husband's face as though she could read his thoughts and interpret them. Then she looked at Philip again. "He still has all his faculties, Mr.

Berg. And if he believes he knows you, then I have no reason to doubt him."

Philip hesitated. There would be no harm in revealing himself to this old man who couldn't speak. But in doing so, he'd also reveal himself to Mrs. Keller, who might eventually tell Felicity. The more people who knew, the more risk there was in word spreading regarding his real identity, and then danger would flock to him faster than vultures to a carcass.

Not only that, but he rather liked being anonymous and having people treat him normally instead of ingratiating themselves or using him for what they could gain. That was one of the reasons why he'd agreed to Declan accompanying him—because he was one of his only friends who wasn't enamored by the fact that he was a prince.

Philip offered Mr. Keller a tight smile and a nod. "I hope you'll forgive me if we don't say anything more about whether or not you recognize me. It's best for all of us if we don't."

Mr. Keller continued to study him, his eyes remaining expressive and conveying a great deal more than Philip had realized was possible. When the older man finally blinked, Philip took that to mean he was acquiescing to Philip's suggestion to put the matter of identities aside.

Philip allowed himself a relieved breath before offering a wider smile. "Now, Mr. Keller, I'd like to provide your wife some respite. Would you mind terribly if I sit with you for a while?"

Immediately Mr. Keller's eyes lit up again with both delight and wonder. And Philip had no doubt the man knew who he was.

As he took the vacated seat and listened to Mrs. Keller's instructions on how to suction out mucus if Mr. Keller should begin to choke, Philip did his best to pretend he was no one special, just as he had all along. But with Mr. Keller's adoring gaze upon him, it was hard to ignore the fact that he was the prince of a nation and that staying in this simple place to be with Felicity Courtney was far from the destiny he'd been born to fulfill.

5

Philip didn't sleep a minute all night long. He spent most of the dark hours with Mr. Keller. When he wasn't spooning in broth or suctioning phlegm, he read to the man from one of the tomes stacked in a pile beside the bed.

Of course, Mr. Keller had chosen the one that was written in Danish, the official language of Lapland. And when Philip easily began to read from the novel in his native tongue, Mr. Keller's eyes seemed to smile in satisfaction.

Mrs. Keller had stumbled into the room midway through the night, yawning and rubbing her eyes, intending to start her usual vigil. But Philip had insisted that she continue to rest, that he and Mr. Keller were getting along fabulously.

The older woman had stared at her husband, who seemed happy and content, before responding with a sob—one that had contained gratefulness and relief. Then she'd returned to the bed in the adjacent room and fallen back asleep.

When she'd bustled in at dawn with her hair combed and wearing a fresh skirt and blouse, Philip guessed he'd given her the best gift anyone had in a long time—a full night's sleep. She'd thanked him quietly, since Mr. Keller had finally dozed off.

Perhaps his aid of the Kellers had begun because he'd wanted to help Felicity. But after spending the time with Mr. Keller, he wished there were more he could do for the poor man and his wife, who were suffering more than most.

His admiration for Felicity had only increased. She'd given this couple a home in a moment of their direst need. And she'd sacrificed herself—even to the point of becoming ill—to bring them some relief.

As the first rays of light broke through the darkness, he sank into the wingback chair next to the sofa where she was still slumbering. He needed to go out and tend to the livestock, haul in more water, and prepare another simple meal.

But for a few minutes, he rewarded himself with the forbidden luxury of staring at Felicity's beautiful face. With her long lashes resting against her pale cheeks and her features relaxed and peaceful, he simply wanted to drink her in. Her hair had come loose and now spread out around her in long, thick waves.

His fingers twitched with the need to test those waves, to let himself sink in and simply bask in the richness. Once finished with her hair—if he ever finished—he'd let himself explore every line of her face, starting at her dainty chin and then her lips.

Her lips. The soft curves, the tiny creases, the delicate dip of her upper lip, the slight parting that beckoned him to taste and explore.

For a moment, his lungs forgot how to work.

She was stunning, even in her sleep. How was it possible for one woman to be so exquisite?

He sat forward, reached out a hand to her cheek, needing to feel her, but paused. If he started something between them, he wouldn't be able to stop. And what if he woke her? What would she do? Let him finish getting his fill of touching her? Or would she sit up and slap his hand away?

No. He couldn't—wouldn't—touch her.

He released a sharp breath, then fell back into his chair, clasping his hands on the arm rests. This wasn't the first time he'd been tempted to touch her, and it probably wouldn't be the last. Regardless, he had to refrain. He was leaving in a few hours, would never see her again, and didn't want to stir up any feelings that shouldn't be.

Doing so would be selfish of him. Very selfish.

He'd reminded himself of that time after time over recent weeks.

He watched her again, the way the blankets molded to her body, the way her arms had captured the blankets, the outline of her long legs. He'd liked so much about her since meeting her, but now, after seeing her here and after learning more about her without her even realizing it, he could almost fancy himself falling in love with her. It was ludicrous. But Felicity Courtney was unlike any other woman he'd ever met.

And he'd known plenty of women over the years. Wherever he'd gone, women had always made themselves available to him, all because of his status as a prince. Of course, he and Declan had women show them attention during the course of their travels too. They were, after all, decently good-looking, single, wealthy men.

But that was one of the first things he'd liked about Felicity—she hadn't sought him out or gawked or fawned over him. He suspected that even if she'd known he was a prince, she still wouldn't have ogled him or changed how she interacted. Even so, he didn't want her to find out, wanted their last memories together to remain untainted by such a discovery.

Maybe he needed to go now, before she awoke, before she realized he was still there and interfering in her business.

Reclining his head, he allowed himself to sink into the cushions of the chair. The truth was, he wanted to see her awake one last time before he left. And he relished witnessing her being peeved at him for staying. In fact, the prospect of a flirtatious spat with her sent his pulse spurting with fresh energy.

He closed his eyes. He'd rest for a short while, then start on the morning chores and bide his time until he finally forced himself to ride away.

Felicity awoke with a start, her eyes flying open. Where was she?

She could tell that she wasn't in her bed in her room off the kitchen. Her face was resting against velvet, her legs were cramped, and her feet brushed against an armrest.

She was on the sofa. Pushing up to her elbows, she grabbed at the blankets as they slid off her body and threatened to fall onto the floor.

A flood of memories came back—those of Philip driving her to the boardinghouse and carrying her inside. He'd placed her upon the sofa and ordered her to stay there, threatening special discipline if she didn't comply.

At the time she'd been too weary to consider what kind of *special* discipline he had in mind, but now her mind filled with the possibilities, particularly those that involved him carrying her just as he had before, but this time pinning her wrists together and then bending in, grazing her cheeks and chin.

The fantasy was so forbidden and unexpected that she flushed. But it didn't matter. Philip didn't matter. He was gone from her life.

He'd never really been in her life to begin with. Just a handsome man on the periphery.

She blinked, trying to put him from her mind and focus on what needed to be done. The soft light filtering in the windows was like that of morning. But that couldn't be. If she'd slept most of the afternoon, then it had to be close to dusk.

Time to get up and finish all the work that Philip hadn't been able to do. As nice as it had been for him to offer to help, she suspected that a man of his class wouldn't know how to manage even half of what she'd listed.

Even so, he'd been right to require her to rest. She'd needed it. And now, she could feel the energy coursing through her in a way it hadn't for a while.

She sat up and swung her legs over. In the same instant, her attention snagged upon the chair beside her and the man in it. Philip.

She froze.

His eyes were closed, and his head rested against the wing portion of the chair. With mussed hair, more errant strands than normal falling into his face, he was breathing deeply, as though he was slumbering.

Why was he sleeping? In her house? In her chair? And why hadn't he gone back to town yet?

Whatever the reason, she wavered on the edge of the couch, uncertain whether to poke his arm and wake him up so that he could be on his way, or whether she ought to let him sleep for a little while.

At the faint throat clearing on the stairs, Felicity's gaze shot to Mrs. Keller only to freeze again at the sight of the woman properly groomed and appearing fresher than she had in a long time, if ever.

Mrs. Keller pressed a finger to her lips and nodded at Philip. Then she glanced up the stairs as though to beckon Felicity upstairs where they could speak without disturbing him.

Felicity almost stood and announced that she refused to give Philip royal treatment. But as she glanced out the window, her thoughts came to a crashing halt. It was most definitely morning. Though the sun seemed to be hidden behind clouds, the brightness was too steady to be anything but daylight.

Did that mean she'd slept all of yesterday afternoon, evening, and night? What time was it now?

Her gaze swung to the small clock on the wall above the sideboard. It was after nine o'clock in the morning.

Ugh. How had she slept so long? She couldn't remember ever sleeping so many hours before.

Mrs. Keller cocked her head toward the upstairs

again, and this time Felicity complied. She followed the older woman up until they were just outside Mr. Keller's bedroom, where she could keep an eye on him.

He seemed to be resting peacefully.

"What happened?" Felicity asked.

"Philip did all of the chores yesterday." Mrs. Keller's whisper was filled with admiration. "He even made me supper."

"Supper? Philip?"

"Yes. Then he stayed with my husband all night and let me sleep."

A strange shiver coursed over Felicity's arms, causing goosebumps. "The whole night?"

"Mr. Keller adores him."

Adores was quite a strong word. Especially in regard to Philip.

"I do believe Mr. Keller recognizes Philip, perhaps from his homeland." She peeked into the room at her husband, as watchful as always for signs that he might be choking. "Mr. Keller emigrated before Philip's lifetime. But perhaps he recognizes a family resemblance in Philip to an old friend."

Felicity had already learned from Mrs. Keller that her husband had emigrated from Lapland, a Scandinavian country, many years ago. The two had met and married not long after Mr. Keller's arrival in Boston, where they'd lived before Mr. Keller had gotten gold fever. They'd moved to the west, first to California and then, in more recent years, to Colorado. They hadn't found much gold, but they'd enjoyed their traveling . . . until Mr. Keller had suffered an apoplexy.

Without children to turn to for help, Mrs. Keller had been doing her best to take care of her husband and manage their small home in Alma. But when funds had run low, she'd finally sold their home and land and made arrangements to move to Denver. They'd come to Fairplay to the Courtney Boardinghouse instead.

Felicity was glad the couple could find refuge with her. She truly was. But she clearly hadn't counted on her body giving out in protest to the lack of sleep.

"If possible, we should allow Philip to rest," Mrs. Keller whispered. "He was such a dear."

It was clear that Philip had easily won over the older couple. He was charming when he put his mind to it—she could give him that. A part of her wanted to let him win her over too. He had stayed and helped. What kind of man would do that? Especially for an invalid like Mr. Keller.

His kindness was jarring her heart loose, and now it tumbled around her chest. But she couldn't let it fall, not for Philip Berg. No matter how nice he'd been over the past day, he was still a wealthy man who was accustomed to playing with the hearts of women. A wealthy man who'd flirted with her for his own amusement. A wealthy man who would take what he wanted and then discard her once the conquest was over.

And the biggest obstacle of them all: he was moving on. He would leave an insignificant and unimportant woman like her behind. Because he didn't need her. Not when he had other women waiting for him at the end of his journey—women who belonged to his class, women who fit into his life, women likely chosen for him by his parents.

Yes, she knew how such people in the upper class truly viewed women like her. She'd already had firsthand experience with rejection. In her last year of living in Pennsylvania, a group of wealthy young women she'd believed to be friends had betrayed her. And the results had hurt, enough that she'd been more than ready to leave Pennsylvania when Charity had suggested they move to the homestead they'd inherited from their uncle.

Felicity had thought being a companion to the wealthy Mrs. Bancroft would be different—that maybe she'd earn some respect in the community, especially with her sister Charity's marriage to a rich Eastern man.

While working for Mrs. Bancroft, she had quickly realized the wealthy lady viewed her as a project, a lump of clay that she'd hoped to fashion into something better. The older woman had seemed to find pleasure in pointing out all of Felicity's flaws, making her feel more deficient than she had before.

Whatever the case, she'd learned once again that she

didn't fit into another social class and that she couldn't aspire to more.

Philip Berg was not the kind of man she was interested in. Not in the least. She would do better with a solid and steady man like Weston Oakley.

Just not now . . .

"So, you'll allow him to sleep a little while longer?" Mrs. Keller asked.

"Yes, of course." It was the least she could do to repay him.

Felicity returned to the front room quietly to find that he was still sleeping as heavily as before. Even if he wasn't the type of man she was interested in, she couldn't keep from pausing and letting herself admire him. She was like a miner examining the mother lode, greedy for every inch of him sprawled out in the chair, his long legs stretched out, his arms crossed, his jaw softened in slumber, and his long lashes dark against his cheeks.

At the sight of his bags and camera equipment by the door, her heart gave an extra beat. He must have gone back into town at some point yesterday and retrieved his belongings. But surely he didn't intend to stay beyond today, did he?

Even if he did linger an extra day or two, he was just passing through in his grand traveling adventures. She couldn't forget that. Absolutely couldn't. Philip Berg would walk out of her life, and she was determined that he wouldn't walk out carrying her heart with him.

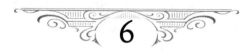

6

The kitchen was one place Felicity never felt the pressure to be perfect.

She blew the liquid on the spoon to cool it and then tasted it. The tang of tomatoes, peppers, basil, and oregano burst on her tongue. She'd learned to make the Italian sauce from Mr. Rosetti, who operated a small restaurant in town. Felicity had easily bonded with the man over their love of cooking.

She leaned against the counter and took a bigger sip. This time she closed her eyes and groaned. "Oh, baby, you're so good."

"I love when you talk about me like that." Philip's voice from the kitchen doorway was low and gravelly.

Her eyes shot open to find him leaning casually against the doorframe, his lids half lowered, his gaze emanating a heat she didn't understand but that caused her cheeks to warm. His hair was messy, as if he'd hastily combed his fingers through it, and his clothes were rumpled.

Even so, he looked as delicious as the sauce, especially with how dark his eyes were and the way they were trained upon her mouth. It was almost as if he were wondering if she could taste him the same way she had the liquid on the spoon.

Taste him? She shook her head. What kind of hussy was she turning into? "I'm not talking about you, Mr. Berg, and you know it."

His lips inched up into a crooked smile. "I could have sworn your nickname for me is *baby*. If not, I won't object if you want to call me that instead of Philip."

"You won't hear either from my lips."

"From your lips?" His gaze again riveted to her mouth. "I like how open you are about discussing your lips and what you'd like to do with them."

Philip Berg was awake and back to his usual war of words and wreaking havoc in her life.

"There is nothing I'm doing with my lips except scolding you." Except, now that they were talking about lips, she couldn't stop herself from looking at his lips. What would it be like to have those lips touch hers?

He started toward her with a devilish gleam in his eyes.

Against her will, anticipation shimmied inside her.

"I'll take a scolding from you any day. Let's hear it."

"Hear what?" She backed up into the stove but then stopped at the heat blazing from inside.

"The scolding you'd like to give me. I can hardly wait." He was fast closing in on her.

She had to find a way to stop him and this interaction. Now. Before she said or did something she'd regret. "You're a scoundrel, Mr. Berg."

Couldn't she think of anything better than that?

With a mental slap, she spun to face the bubbling pot on the stove and breathed in the aroma of the sauce as she busied herself stirring.

When he halted behind her, close enough for her to hear his breathing, her stirring slowed to a crawl and her body tightened, feeling his presence as if he were already touching her.

What was he doing?

"Are you giving out tastes?" The whisper brushed near her ear and neck.

Oh, dear heavens. Her eyes closed involuntarily. Delectable heat zinged along every nerve ending—nerve endings that wanted his whisper and his breath to keep on caressing her. Everything about this man affected her much more than she wanted it to, much more than she dared to admit. He made her feel alive and excited and slightly off-kilter, as if she never knew what to expect from him.

And she liked it.

With a huff, she started stirring again. Why? Why couldn't she feel this way about Weston Oakley? A man who cherished her and considered her an equal and wanted her to be a part of his life. A man who cared for her enough to rearrange his life to be with her. A man who desired her so much that he wouldn't leave her the first opportunity he had.

She sidled away from the stove and away from Philip's mesmerizing presence. As she took a step away from him, she realized she'd taken the spoon with her and now it was dripping onto the floor. Regardless, she held it out like a weapon, needing him to keep his distance so that she could clear her head.

"The only taste you'll get is at supper."

His gaze raked her mouth. "I'll take it."

"A taste of the sauce, and nothing more."

His eyes widened with fake innocence. "You're not planning to cook any pasta to go with the sauce?"

She couldn't keep her smile back any longer. "You're too much."

He held open his arms, drawing attention to his broad chest that strained against the buttons of his shirt. "This"—he waved a hand toward himself—"is never too much."

She could agree that he had the kind of body and face no one would ever tire of looking at. But she wouldn't say so to him. He was already puffed up enough and didn't need her adding to his arrogance.

She had to bring the conversation under her control. She moved toward the worktable, which was littered with the remains of the vegetables and herbs she'd chopped. "Thank you for all that you've done to help."

"You're welcome." His voice held a seriousness and sincerity she hadn't expected.

She gathered up a handful of peelings and leafy tops and dropped them into a compost bucket. "I was surprised to wake up and find you still here."

"I was glad I could help."

"The sleep was just what Mrs. Keller and I both needed."

"Good. I hadn't thought about that." His tone was laced with teasing. "I was simply enjoying spending time with Mr. Keller. He's a nice fellow."

She swept more leftovers into the bucket. "He's a very smart man, even if he can't express himself."

"It's clear he's attempting to make the most of his life." He crossed to the opposite side of the worktable and began to gather up the bowls and silverware she'd used in making the garlic bread now rising in a warm spot on the stove.

"It was kind of you to spend the entire night. You'll be tired later."

"Not me. A few hours of slumber in an uncomfortable and too-small chair has made me into a new person."

She smiled as she swiped up a dishrag and began to wipe the counter. "And thank you for taking care of the chores yesterday and last night. I appreciate that too."

"Of course. I'm always happy when I can make a woman's dreams come true." He winked.

And there he was, his annoying self again. "I admit, I was surprised to discover you were capable of completing any chores, especially anything that required you to use your muscles." She would have liked to have seen him chopping wood. All his brawn would have been a magnificent sight to behold.

He carried the dirty dishes to the sink. "So, you're thinking about my muscles?"

"No, of course not." She had been, but she snorted and changed the subject. "I suppose you're anxious to leave just as soon as you can?"

"I'm surprised you haven't kicked me out the front door yet."

He'd avoided answering her question. Why? Did he want to stay? "I didn't have the heart to kick you out when you were sleeping so comfortably."

This time he didn't acknowledge her effort at teasing, not with a nod or grin or laugh. Instead, he rolled up his shirt sleeves, almost as if he didn't quite know what to say.

The more the silence dragged, the tighter her chest drew.

He pushed his sleeves past his elbows, then reached
for a kettle on the stove and dumped warm water into the
sink and over the dishes. When he picked up the bar of
soap at the back of the sink and began to lather a rag, she
couldn't stand aside and watch him any longer. She
huffed and then strode toward him.

Before he could move out of reach, she snatched the
soap from his hand.

He paused, the soapy dishrag poised above the first
bowl. She could almost see his mind at work trying to
figure out what she was up to. Clearly not having a clue,
he began scrubbing.

She lunged for the dishrag.

As though he'd been anticipating her move, he lifted
the dripping rag up over their heads.

She jumped for it, latched onto the bottom, and
started to draw it away.

He extended his hand higher, moving it out of her
grasp.

"Give me the rag." She hopped again, clasped his arm,
and tried to drag it down.

He watched her useless effort and quirked a brow. "If
you want to feel my strong arms, all you need to do is ask.
I'll gladly allow it."

Her hand spread over the solidness of his upper arm.
She couldn't get her fingers to fit around his entire bicep.
Even so, she released a scoffing sound. "For a second, I

thought I was holding on to a baby goat—"

With a grin, he flexed, the muscles popping even more.

He was all strength and sinew with no baby goat in sight. Her fingers betrayed her with the need to linger, to relish the ripple of his muscles. But if she wanted to maintain any dignity, she had to keep a clear head. She dropped her hand and stood back, clutching the bar of soap. "You're free to go."

His gaze snapped to her, surprise filling his eyes.

She fisted her hands on her hips and glared at him. She didn't want him doing her dishes and then walking out her door. He could leave now, and she'd take care of the dishes all on her own.

He didn't lower the dishrag, still held it above his head, water dripping slowly to the floor. "What if I'm not ready to go yet?"

Why wouldn't he be ready? It was past the noon hour. He'd need to get into town, secure his passage for the stagecoach, and make sure he was on the last ride out for the night. If he missed today, he'd only leave tomorrow.

His eyes held hers and this time contained no mirth. The blue was as dark and serious as a deep well. "I'll help you again tonight, stay with Mr. Keller, let you and Mrs. Keller sleep."

"Why?" She lifted her chin, not caring that her tone

was demanding. "What difference will one more night make?"

He opened his mouth to respond, but for once, he didn't say anything witty or playful or seductive. He clamped his lips closed and dropped the dishrag into the sink before taking a step back. "I shall ride into town and see if I can finish finding you the help you need."

"I can take care of that myself."

"I know." His voice grew solemn. "But I'd like to do it. If you'll allow me."

She wanted to tell him no. To ride away and never come back. But something about the way he stood stiffly, almost sadly, gave her pause.

Was he reluctant to leave?

Her heart gave an extra thud at the prospect, but then just as quickly, she forced her pulse to beat at the regular pace. "Mr. Berg, I don't want you to delay on account of me any longer."

"I'm the one dragging my feet in leaving." The admission was soft and his eyes warm.

This time when her heart sputtered faster, she allowed it. For all of three seconds. Then she reined it in with a hard jerk. "You shouldn't stay, not when you know it's only postponing the inevitable."

He hesitated, then gave a curt nod. "You really do need the help here. When I'm making my traveling arrangements, I'll do some checking around and see if anyone is interested in your advertisement."

He was being sincere. She could be sincere too, couldn't she? "Thank you. If you want to take the wagon, I can walk into town later today or tomorrow and retrieve it."

"No, I'll locate someone to drive it back." He rubbed his hand over the scruff on his jaw, looked everywhere in the kitchen but at her. Finally, he shot a glance at her. "You're someone special, Felicity Courtney. And I've been privileged to meet you."

She wanted to find something to say in farewell, words about coming to visit again, or writing her a letter, or not forgetting about her. But she bit them back. What was the use in encouraging any future communication?

"Goodbye, Mr. Berg." It was best to keep this parting short and to the point.

She placed the soap back on the sink. Then she picked up the wooden spoon she'd been using to stir the sauce and returned to the pot on low heat at the back of the stovetop. She circled the spoon inside unseeingly, her mind envisioning Philip sleeping on the chair beside her this morning, so good-looking.

Behind her, she could feel him watching her, perhaps even waiting for her to turn around and face him one more time. But she refrained and kept stirring, rooted to the spot in front of the stove.

After achingly long seconds, she heard him plod out

of the kitchen. He headed up the stairs, and although she couldn't hear his conversation with the Kellers, she guessed he was telling them goodbye. When his footsteps descended, she held her breath, waiting for him to enter the kitchen and speak with her again, perhaps tell her he'd changed his mind and intended to remain.

But his steps veered toward the front door.

Her spoon grew idle in the thickening sauce. She could hear him pause, likely picking up his bags, then he opened the door, stepped outside, and closed it behind him, quietly, with only a click.

She leaned the spoon against the rim of the pot, pivoted, and started toward the doorway. She wanted to chase after him and say a real goodbye, maybe give him a hug, maybe thank him again for his help the previous night. But she grabbed onto the worktable to halt herself.

A moment later, as the wagon creaked and rumbled on its way past the house, she refused to look out the window at Philip passing by. Finally, when the sound of the wagon faded into the distance, she walked into the front room and plopped down onto the sofa with a huff of frustration.

Good riddance. She was glad Philip Berg was finally out of her life. He'd put her on edge since the very first moment she'd seen him at their first dinner together at Mrs. Bancroft's, although she could admit his witty remarks and banter had been a welcome relief from the usual boring conversations.

As she stared out the window—certainly not with the hope that she'd see him returning—her attention snagged upon a square item sitting beside the door.

It couldn't be.

She stood and crossed to it.

Oh, but it was.

She knelt beside the box, slipped the metal clip loose, then carefully opened the lid. There, inside a case of black velvet, sat his camera.

She fingered the wooden top, the folded leather bellows, and then the lens.

Her gaze swept over the area by the door. It was empty. He'd taken everything else, including the tripod.

So how had he forgotten this?

Her heart pattered with a sudden thrill. Did that mean he'd have to come back for it? And if he did, what would she say or do differently?

"No." She whispered the word harshly.

She flipped the camera case lid closed, secured the hook in place, and then stood.

She didn't want a man in her life right now. And if she did, she wouldn't want one who came back for a camera. She'd want a man who came back for her.

7

Philip rolled the wagon to a stop in front of the sawmill. The gray clouds overhead had begun to spit rain, and the temperature was quickly dropping.

He'd spent the better part of the afternoon searching for a hired hand for Felicity, but he hadn't liked any of the men he'd interviewed. Not a single one.

As a result, he'd been left with no other choice but to ride out to Weston Oakley's spread and ask him to go over each day and help Felicity. Even if Philip didn't think the fellow was right for a woman like Felicity, he was the best option. He was kind and considerate and cared enough about her that he wouldn't take advantage of her.

Even so, as Philip studied first the sawmill and then the grain mill farther upriver, he couldn't stop jealousy from slicing through him. The mills were neat and organized, both tall wooden buildings in good repair, the waiting wagons lined up in an orderly fashion, mill hands working diligently, hefting heavy loads of cut timber or bags of milled grain into the waiting wagons.

Had he hoped for worse? That Weston's businesses would be ramshackle and rundown? That he'd have an excuse not to involve Weston in Felicity's life after all?

The tall, dark-haired man wasn't in sight—not around the mills and not down the tree-lined lane that led to what appeared to be a fairly new home that had to be Weston's. Of course, it was nothing like the palatial residences his family lived in, but it was a fine home for the high country—two stories with a wrap-around porch, painted a light yellow, with plenty of big windows. Behind it sat a decent-sized barn and large paddock with a number of horses and steers.

A dog lying on the porch lifted its head at the sight of Philip, but then must have decided he wasn't a threat and rested his head back on outstretched front legs.

If Weston wasn't available, Philip would have no choice but to ride away, his mission to hire help for Felicity unfulfilled. And then he'd be obliged to return to her boardinghouse for another night. He couldn't in good conscience leave her to fend for herself a moment longer than she already had.

The problem was, Felicity was right about his leaving. If he went back and kept dragging his feet, he was only postponing the unavoidable departure—if not for

Denver, then for someplace else after that.

To make matters worse, the longer he stayed, the more he risked putting her into danger. Any association with him had to remain short and shallow and superficial. That was what he'd been trying for all along. But somehow with her, it hadn't been enough.

With a sigh, he hopped down from the wagon, the ground beginning to grow slushy with the rain that was now falling harder and contained the sting of ice. He approached an older fellow who had the look of someone in charge. After inquiring about Weston, he learned the boss had ridden up to a new mill he'd recently purchased in a nearby mining town and wouldn't be back until tomorrow.

Philip instructed the mill worker to pass along a message—that upon returning, Weston needed to start helping at Felicity's boardinghouse. Then Philip hopped back up onto his wagon, his mind made up. He had no choice but to stay one more night with Felicity.

He veered the wagon south, his heart suddenly lighter. Another night wouldn't cause any trouble in the scope of things. Declan would be fine without him.

After riding only a short distance away from the mills, the rain began falling with increased intensity . . . and it started to freeze over everything, covering the trees, brush, and wagon road.

His garments, already damp, quickly became

saturated, chilling him to his bones. A sheen of ice soon slicked over his hat and coat and his gloves so that he could hardly bend his fingers to hold on to the reins. The old gelding slipped and slid, and the wagon twisted back and forth.

Finally, after nearly falling, the horse stopped and refused to budge. The clouds hung low in the sky and continued to pour out a mixture of rain and ice with no sign of stopping. As Philip descended from the wagon and his feet touched the ground, he slipped and almost landed on his backside. Only his quick reflexes and grabbing on to the wagon kept him from going down.

The barren wilderness spread all around—the foothills covered in tufts of dried grass, brown shrubs, and a few trees that had lost their leaves. The clouds obscured the mountain peaks and seemed to be rolling in even faster, stormy and dark and loaded with more precipitation.

He'd be better off heading directly for Felicity's boardinghouse rather than going into town first. He didn't know the distance that remained, but he needed to push forward.

He inched his way toward the front of the gelding. He had no choice but to lead the creature on foot. As he grabbed onto the horse's bit and gathered the lead line, he used both to stabilize himself even as more ice pelted him.

After long moments of coaxing, he managed to get

the horse moving again, but the pace was slow and unsteady.

An uneasiness nagged at him. If he weren't careful, he might not make it to the boardinghouse, might even end up stranded in the foothills until the storm passed through. Then again, with the cold air blowing against him and as wet as he was, he could easily freeze if he didn't find shelter.

At some point, the wind picked up, making his trek even more treacherous and miserable. He tried to use the gelding to block the pelting ice, tried to draw warmth from the creature. But nothing could protect him from the storm's growing intensity.

By the time he stumbled down the lane that led to the boardinghouse, he couldn't feel his fingers or toes. The rest of his flesh was numb, his eyelashes were crusted nearly closed, and ice clung to the layer of hair on his chin and cheeks.

He knew he needed to take the horse to the barn, where it would be safe and out of the storm, but at the sight of the light in the front window, he could only think of one thing: warmth.

Sliding on the ice-covered front steps, he managed to make it up and to the door. He couldn't move his arm to bang and instead thudded the door with his boot.

A moment later, the door opened a crack to reveal Felicity. It had been less than six hours since he'd ridden away, but at the sight of her delicate features creased with wariness, he felt as though he'd been away from her for six years.

He tried to get a word out, but he couldn't make his lips work. Instead, he wavered, feeling as though he was about to lose consciousness.

She swung the door wide, and the wariness quickly changed to worry. "I knew you would miss me, but you didn't need to come out in a storm to see me again."

He tried for a smile, but again, he was too weak.

"Confound it, Philip." Her voice took on a sudden edge, and she grabbed hold of his coat and dragged him inside. "You're frozen."

The warmth of the front room surrounded him, but with his garments stuck to his skin, he was going to need more than a warm room to thaw him out.

At her pause and glance outside past him, he shook his head, hoping to warn her against going out to care for the horse. He didn't want her to battle the ice or to risk slipping and falling. Besides, he would take care of the horse and wagon as soon as he gained back some feeling.

But he couldn't say any of that, was too weak and cold to be coherent.

She closed the door behind him, all the while assessing him. "We need to get you out of your frozen clothing."

He could think of about a dozen comebacks to her

statement, but again, he couldn't get his voice to work and had instead started to chatter uncontrollably.

She began to work on the buttons on his coat, but the ice was too thick. With a mutter of frustration, she moved to his gloves. But they, too, were frozen and wouldn't slide off.

"Hurry." She nudged him toward the kitchen, her voice taking on an edge of urgency. Somehow he managed to cross the room and move into the kitchen, which was warmer than the front room. She pulled a chair up to the stove, tugged him down into it, and then added more wood to the fire already blazing inside.

Once the flames were crackling and sparking with renewed heat, she held his hands toward the fire. As the ice rapidly melted, she wiggled his fingers free of the frozen glove, dropping first one and then the other to the floor before taking both of his hands between hers and rubbing and blowing on them.

He was too numb, still too frozen to appreciate her touch. All he could think about was that he was cold—so deeply cold—that he couldn't stop shaking.

She labored over his boots and socks next, peeling off the frozen items until his red and raw feet were exposed. Like his hands, she rubbed and blew and let the heat of the fire start to bring a tingling back into his skin.

She'd already cast aside his hat at some point. And now she started on his coat, the ice on the buttons finally gone so that she could divest him of the wool that was nothing more than a slab of ice. As she tossed it aside, she paused at the buttons of his shirt.

The creases in her forehead were adorable, as were the crinkles at the corners of her eyes. Her lush lips were pursed together, as though she was holding back a blistering tongue-lashing. He wished she'd speak her mind, wanted to hear her voice, could think of nothing better than listening to a tirade from her.

His teeth were still chattering, and now his fingers and toes tingled with shards of pain.

She started to back away from his shirt.

"Do it." His voice came out hoarse.

Her startled gaze met his, and a flush filled her cheeks. She returned her fingers to his top button but hesitated.

"You have to . . . even though it will be . . . impossible to keep your hands off me . . ." The words were raspy, but he hoped she could hear his teasing and realize he was trying to lighten the mood.

Her lips curved just slightly. "Yes, at this moment I can hardly think of anything but wanting to run my fingers over your icy flesh. It's so enticing."

"I know . . . I am enticing, even at my worst."

She fumbled with the first few buttons but then made quick work of the last several.

"You're good at that." His voice came out more clearly. "Maybe I should have you do it more often."

She finished the last one, then stood back and glared at him, fist on her hip. "I liked it better when you were too frozen to talk."

"No, you didn't."

"Yes, believe me, I did."

His face was thawing, and the life was beginning to rush through him—his relief at having made it to safety coupled with the relief at seeing her again. How had he believed he could ride away from her and never see her again?

She wrestled with his wet, stiff shirt sleeve, trying to drag it down his arm. He couldn't keep from simply staring and watching her.

Her red hair was coiled up elegantly with a strand loose on either side of her face. She was still wearing the white blouse and plain skirt that she'd had on in the kitchen earlier, but the collar of the shirt was now unbuttoned and hung open, revealing her long, graceful neck.

Her cheeks were flushing more with every passing moment that she attempted to extract him from his clothing. From embarrassment or from the heat that was emanating from the stove?

She was finally able to get one sleeve off and stood back. "There."

He glanced down at the other half of his shirt, still frozen and clinging to his body. "You're not nearly done.

After the shirt, you have to take off my pants."

She gasped and then lightly smacked him in the chest. "Absolutely not."

He chuckled, but it ended on a cough.

"I would say the cold has addled your brain, but it was already addled."

He laughed again, but this time erupted into a fit of coughing, his lungs still working to thaw out too.

At the sound of his hacking, she returned to his second sleeve and set to work sliding it off with the same effort she'd used on the other, until he was free and wearing only an undershirt—which was wet and clung to his body too.

She disappeared into the little room off the kitchen that she used as a bedroom and came out a moment later, her arms piled with blankets. "Are your hands thawed yet?"

He wiggled his fingers and winced at the pain. "Slowly."

"How did you get caught out in the storm?" She draped one of the blankets over his shoulders, then knelt in front of him with another blanket and began wrapping it around his feet.

The question seemed innocent enough, but something in her tone told him the answer was important to her. "I rode out to see Weston Oakley."

She paused and narrowed her eyes at him. "Why?"

How could he tell her about his failed efforts to locate her help without coming across as a deranged lunatic? He wasn't sure it was possible. "I spent most of the afternoon trying to find a fellow to fill your advertisement."

She sat back on her heels. "Most of the afternoon?"

"And I couldn't find anyone I liked."

"I find it difficult to believe that after an entire afternoon you couldn't find anyone."

"Not one."

"Maybe you were being too picky."

"Of course I was being picky. I don't think you should have just anyone coming out here and helping."

"You do know I can fend for myself?" She rose to her feet and fisted her hands on her hips.

He shrugged. "I abhor the thought that you would need to fend off anyone. Thus, I decided Weston is the best choice."

She opened her mouth as if to say something in protest. Then she halted and clamped her lips closed. From everything Philip had witnessed, she seemed to like Weston, but she wasn't enamored with him. If rumors were true, Weston had already proposed numerous times. And she'd turned him down every single time.

Weston clearly wasn't deterred and would probably wear her out with all his asking so that eventually she'd marry him. Maybe she knew it. Maybe that was why she wasn't offering more of an objection to his plan to have Weston help her.

"I drove out to the mills to ask Weston to start coming by every day, but he wasn't there."

"I don't want to bother Weston."

"Believe me, that man wants to be *bothered* by you." Every man wanted to be *bothered* by Felicity Courtney.

She shoved Philip again, this time his arm, and he had the urge to swipe her hand and drag her down on his lap, pull her in, and then taste the rosy flush in her cheeks before bending lower and tasting her neck and even the little bit of collarbone showing where her blouse was unbuttoned.

Just the prospect sent warmth through his veins to his fingers and toes.

"So after you left Weston's mills, why didn't you go to Fairplay? It's closer. You could have made it there without freezing off every single one of your limbs."

He hugged the blanket closer, his wet undershirt making him shiver. "Do you want the truth?" He couldn't keep his voice from dropping a note with seriousness.

She grew stiff, as though afraid of his answer. "Yes, of course. I prefer only the truth." The wariness from a short while ago was back in her countenance.

Did he dare admit that he'd wanted to see her again? Why not? "If you really must know, I came because I couldn't bear the thought of you going without help for a single night."

"Oh." She barely breathed the word.

"And I wanted the chance to see you one more time."

As soon as the words were out, the flames within the stove seemed to burst higher, making the room hot and the tension crackle. He'd said what he shouldn't have, but for a reason he didn't understand, he couldn't make himself regret it.

And what about her? What did she think of his bold confession?

She narrowed her eyes. "So you didn't return because you forgot something?"

"Is this a trick question?"

"No."

"I forgot to kiss you goodbye?"

"Did you?"

His attention locked onto her lips. "Yes. And I'd like to rectify that right now." Indeed, he would. Very much so. But he was well enough versed in banter to know that saying and doing were two different things. And even though he was teasing her about kissing, he wouldn't actually go through with it.

She just shook her head while a smile hovered over her lips—a smile that made him want to scoop her up and let his fingers trace her lips.

"What else did you forget?" she persisted.

"You?" Melting ice dripped off his hair onto the blanket.

"Of your belongings?" Her tone filled with false exasperation.

He catalogued his bags that were still in the back of the wagon. Clearly she was still testing him. "Since I keep failing your quiz, why don't you tell me what I forgot."

"Then you really don't know?" Her brown eyes brimmed with the usual intensity that he found too enticing.

He'd already made a fool of himself. Why stop now? "I didn't forget anything, Felicity. I wish I had—then I'd have a noble excuse for being here instead of the simple fact that I wanted to see you again."

She was quiet for several heartbeats. "You shouldn't have come."

"I know. But I'm glad I did anyway."

This time her smile came out in full force, lighting up her eyes and making him momentarily breathless. He'd passed her test and made her happy. And that was something he wanted to keep on doing.

She reached for her cloak on a peg near the back door, then tossed him a saucy look. "Now that you're half undressed, you won't be able to stop me from going outside and taking care of the horse and wagon."

The humor drained away.

With a smug smile, she opened the back door, and a gust of icy wind blew inside.

He lunged toward her. "I'll be warmed up in a

moment and will do it—"

She was already stepping out and closing the door behind her.

He reached for his shirt where she'd dropped it on the floor. It was still stiff with cold and ice.

The door banged open again, and she poked her head inside, her cheeks now red and her eyes flashing. "If you dare step a foot outside, I won't give you back your camera."

"My camera?"

"You left it here." It was her turn to wink at him as he so often did with her. And she did so with slow exaggeration before wrestling the door closed again.

As soon as she was gone, he lowered himself into the chair. Then he laughed. Felicity was unlike any other woman he'd ever known, never afraid to speak her mind, put him in his place, and dole out to him the same measure of teasing that he gave her.

If he searched the whole world over, he knew he'd never find another woman like her. In fact, he *had* traveled much of the world and had never met anyone who compared with Felicity Courtney.

Was there a way he could keep her in his life? Was it possible that someday—after he was no longer running for his life—he could reconnect with her?

He hadn't wanted to consider the possibility of Felicity being in his future. He hadn't wanted to raise false hopes between them. And he hadn't wanted to contemplate any relationship when he didn't know if he'd live past tomorrow.

But with everything he'd given up, maybe he could allow himself this one wishful dream—the dream where he made it out of his nightmare alive and could be with Felicity again.

Maybe it was a reckless dream—one he'd eventually regret. But for now, he wanted to enjoy a last evening with her before he had to go.

8

Felicity lit the last candle on the dining room table, then stood back and admired her beautiful meal. A serving bowl with the homemade pasta and sauce sat beside the basket of garlic bread. On the opposite side of the candles, she'd placed a salad of greens with radishes, carrots, and peppers. She'd also baked an apple pie earlier in the afternoon and had given it a prominent position on the table.

Not to impress Philip. Why would she want to do that?

Philip had offered to take a plate of the meal to Mrs. Keller when he'd gone up to his room to change.

The firm thud of footsteps overhead made Felicity tingle with awareness of Philip's presence. He was here. Really here. And he had a room now, which made his visit seem even more official.

She still couldn't believe it and pinched herself to

make sure she wasn't dreaming.

After she'd returned from taking care of Stan and the wagon, she'd carried Philip's bags into the house against his adamant protest that he would do it later. The ice on the grass and gravel had made maneuvering difficult, and in attempting to walk only the short distance to the barn and back, she'd nearly fallen a dozen times. How had Philip gone several miles?

She'd scolded Philip thoroughly for daring such a trek. Thankfully, he'd remained by the stove, thawing out little by little. Now that he had his belongings—which had mostly stayed dry in his canvas bag—he was changing his clothing while she set the table for supper.

She eyed the candles. Did they make the meal look too romantic? She didn't want Philip to think she was interested in him, because she wasn't, even though he'd admitted to coming back simply to see her and not for his camera. In fact, he hadn't even realized he'd left his camera behind.

A thin ribbon of delight wove through her again, as it had when she'd probed him earlier. His arrival was because of her and no other reason.

He was turning out to be an honest man, one full of integrity. In addition, he was kind and thoughtful. What other man would spend an entire afternoon trying to locate help for her? Weston certainly hadn't. To be fair, Weston had offered to come for himself. But still, Philip had taken the time to seek out men, interview them, and try to find someone reliable for her.

At the heavy patter of steps in the hallway nearing the stairway, she combed a hand over loose hairs before brushing at her simple blouse and then at her skirt. She'd already taken off her apron and stowed it in the kitchen. Part of her wished she'd donned one of the elegant dresses that Charity had left behind for her. She wore them for trips into town. But whenever she was working around the homestead, she donned the plain clothing that she'd grown up wearing.

Although she could appreciate the values and simple faith of the Quakers, she hadn't lamented when her parents had broken away from their community. She'd been ready to experience more of the world. That's why she'd been eager for friendship with the wealthy young ladies who had included her in their activities during that last year in Pennsylvania. Though the friendship had turned out to be a disaster, Felicity had learned a great deal about what life was like outside the Quaker society.

She'd also learned a great deal while living as Mrs. Bancroft's companion. Even if the time had been difficult and the woman had been demeaning, Felicity had enjoyed all the things that had once been forbidden— music, dancing, games, parties, and fancy clothing. Especially the fancy clothing. She hadn't gotten to travel with Mrs. Bancroft the way she'd hoped, but she'd met interesting people from other places around the world, like Philip.

Now, as Philip loped down the stairs in dry garments, a warm sputter pulsed through her—one charged with strange energy. His blond hair was dark from being damp, but he'd combed it back into lazy waves. He'd put on wool trousers and thick socks. His shirt was a warm flannel and not one of the immaculate white dress shirts he'd worn to the dinner parties at Mrs. Bancroft's.

He'd always been incredibly handsome in his evening attire. But this casual, shoeless version of him was even better.

As he reached the bottom of the stairs, he slanted a grin at her, one that tilted her and the world around her. He had such a devilishly handsome smile.

He paused and rubbed his hands together, unable to conceal a shiver.

"Are you still cold?" She crossed to the stove by the sofa, intending to add more fuel and take the chill out of the air—a chill that the gusting wind continued to push in through every crack of the house. It had been less than two hours since his arrival, but the darkness of evening had fallen and brought with it dropping temperatures.

Before she could toss more wood into the stove, he stepped into her way and grabbed her arm. "I'm just fine. And I don't want you behaving as my servant any longer."

Her attention fixed on his long fingers easily

encompassing her wrist and pulling her back. "I'm not your servant."

"I should think not." His thumb brushed against her pulse, which was suddenly thrumming against her skin loud and fast, as if wanting to break free.

Oh, dear heavens. She began to tug away from him before she acted irrationally and did something stupid like throw herself at him, press her body wantonly against him, and wrap her arms around him.

He released her hand only to capture it again and situate it in the crook of his arm. "You're a lady and should have a whole castle full of servants at your beck and call."

"Castle full?" She tried not to think about how good his muscles felt against her fingertips. "I take it you live in a castle with an army of servants?" She wasn't sure why she was more curious about him tonight. Maybe it was the prospect of a candlelit dinner. Maybe it was the fact that he was here instead of on his way to Denver. Maybe it was the intimate meal ahead with just the two of them.

Whatever it was, she wanted to know more about this man.

He led her to the table as regally as if they really were a lord and lady living in a castle. As he pulled out her chair and helped her push it in, she waited almost breathlessly for him to take his spot across from her.

As he sat down, she watched him expectantly. "Well?"

"The meal looks stunning." He swept his gaze over everything, appreciation lighting his eyes.

"You're ignoring my question."

"The question about whether or not I'm happy to see you again?" He unfolded his napkin and laid it in his lap. "You needn't fish for compliments so blatantly."

She scooted the pasta bowl toward him so that he'd dish up his serving first. Exactly how happy was he to see her again? She wanted to ask, but she couldn't, or he'd have the advantage over her. And she couldn't allow that. "I suppose the question you should be asking is whether I'm happy to see you."

In the middle of dipping the fork into the pasta, he paused. "How could you not be happy to see my adorable face again?"

"Adorable?" She glanced around the room as though looking for someone. "Did you bring Declan with you this time?"

His grin played upon his lips as he heaped a mound of pasta and sauce upon his plate. "Just admit I'm more adorable than Declan."

She paused and pretended to think about it. Then she shrugged playfully. "You're right. I usually reserve the word adorable for describing baby chicks and newborn bunnies. But I guess it applies to you too."

For a short while as they ate, they kept the banter flying, neither one letting it drop. The exchange, as usual, invigorated her and sent secret thrills whispering to every region of her body, bringing her to life. Time with him always made her feel alive, but she never quite understood why.

His eyes seemed alive too. Thankfully his frozenness had melted away, and he was moving and talking and carrying on just as he normally did.

"Thank you for this exquisite meal." He swallowed a last bite. "That was kind of you to make it especially for me, in the event I returned."

"Yes, of course, I plan all my meals around fickle guests."

"If not for me, then why else would you go to so much trouble?"

"I wanted something special for Mrs. Keller." She savored the strong flavors of the sauce that had blended and cooked all afternoon, filling the house even now with its tantalizing aroma.

"So I rank below Mrs. Keller in how special I am?"

"Only truly special people get any ranking in my list."

"Then obviously I'm truly special."

"No. You have to be humble."

"I'm very humble."

She quirked a brow at him.

He gave her a lopsided grin that easily tore down all her defenses—not that she had many up. Even so, she had a strange longing to move beyond their bantering and find out more about him. "Since you're so humble, tell me about your humble origins."

He sopped up sauce into a piece of the garlic bread. For a moment, he remained silent, almost as though he was contemplating ignoring her again. Finally, he popped the piece of bread in his mouth, chewed it, then shrugged. "Let's make a deal. Every time I divulge a piece of my background, you have to do the same."

"I ask you one question, then you get to reciprocate with a question of your own. Five questions only. We give each other straight and honest answers. No avoidance allowed."

"Are there any limits to the queries?" he asked.

"Do you want limits?" She had nothing to hide, but that didn't mean the same was true of him.

"Why don't we give each other the ability to pass on one question?"

"I won't need that, but if you do, then I'll agree to it."

"We'll see about that." He leaned back in his chair, the candlelight dancing over his prominent features and highlighting his fair hair that had finally dried. It was mussed and hung over his forehead. The light-blue flecks of his eyes were rimmed with darker blue that pulled her in and threatened to knock her off her feet like a tidal wave.

"Do you want the honor of asking the first question? Or would you like me to go first?" Her pulse swirled erratically, even though she didn't want it to.

He gave a brief regal bow of his head. "My lady, as a gentleman, I can do nothing less than allow you the privilege of beginning the inquisition."

"Inquisition? Is that how you see this?"

"Yes." He smiled almost wickedly. "Now my turn."

"I thought you were allowing me to go first."

"You did."

"I did not."

"You asked me if I saw the questions as an inquisition, and I said yes."

She scoffed. "You're cheating, Mr. Berg. Clearly you have something to hide, or you wouldn't shirk your fair share of questions."

He held his arms open wide as though he had nothing to hide. "I'm all yours. Ask away."

She'd never tire of the easy way they could relate to one another. She had Philip here tonight all to herself—with Mr. and Mrs. Keller in the room above, likely listening to every word of their conversation. Nevertheless, she needed to go deeper with him. Wanted to know more, needed to know more.

She tapped at her lip. If she only had four questions left, then she had to make them count. "Tell me all about your family, your parents, siblings, grandparents, anyone else important to you."

"That's not a question. That's a command."

With an exasperated sigh, she rolled her eyes. "What is your family like, including your parents, siblings, grandparents, and anyone else important to you?"

He hesitated only a little before telling her that his dad had passed away two years ago of a lung disease. He mentioned an older brother Gustaf, who had gotten married a year or so past, but didn't seem keen on discussing the fellow, and she got the impression that perhaps a rift existed between them.

Philip was much more eager to talk about his younger sister Estelle, who was eighteen and sounded as spirited as he was. He seemed to have a loving relationship with his mother and grandmother and regarded both of them highly.

His question to her was very much the same—an inquiry into her family. He listened attentively as she shared about the death of their parents to influenza, and about her two sisters: Charity, who'd married Hudson Vanderwater a few months ago and was residing with him in the East until the spring, and then Patience, who'd recently wedded an English gentleman rancher, Spencer Wolcott, and moved to his ranch.

The third and fourth questions were similar in nature—questions about their childhoods and faith and family bonds and what it had been like growing up in their homes. Again, Philip answered seriously but hesitantly when it came to discussing his brother. But she learned a little more about his growing up in Lapland and had the sense from the way he described his travels and life that he'd most definitely had a privileged upbringing with a wealthy family.

When it came time for the fifth question, Felicity took her time in thinking of what she most wanted to know about Philip. And one question nagged her more than any other.

He leaned back in his chair across the dining room table and sipped a cup of coffee she'd percolated, his eyes upon her, half filled with mischief and half serious. "What is the last secret you want to squeeze from me tonight?"

The wind rattled the windowpanes and whistled in the stovepipe. From what she'd been able to tell when she'd gotten up to make the coffee while Philip refueled the stoves and checked on the Kellers, the ice had turned to snow, which was now falling quite heavily.

"Hmmm . . ." She took a drink from her own cup of strong, black brew.

Even as she searched her mind for a last good question, she kept returning to the need to know more about what he wanted from his future, particularly if he had plans for marriage. But if she asked, he would be sure to tease her about having ulterior motives, possibly even accuse her of wanting him for herself.

"Come now, ask me whatever you're dying to know."

Over the rim of his cup, his gaze lingered almost languidly on her features. There was nothing in his gaze that was inappropriate or that even showed desire, but she felt something nonetheless. It felt like a tug against her stomach, low and hot.

She ignored the feeling and forced the last question. "What have your relationships with women both now and in the past been like?"

As expected, a slow grin worked its way up his lips. "You're trying to find out if I like you?"

"No. I already know you like me." She blew on the hot liquid in her mug and took a tiny sip.

He drank too, letting his gaze stay locked with hers. He didn't bother denying her, but neither did he acknowledge that what she'd said was true.

"So?" she persisted.

"Are you certain you'd like to use your last question on my relationship history?"

"Yes."

He set his mug down. "How far back do you want me to go?"

"To the beginning."

One of his brows shot up. "To the girl I kissed when I was a lad of ten?"

Did she really want to hear about all the women he'd had over the years? No doubt he'd consorted with many, especially since both charm and appeal were as second nature to him as breathing. Actually listening to him rattle off the many women he'd kissed or slept with wouldn't be a pleasurable way to spend any amount of time.

"Start with your most serious relationship."

He hesitated, as though thinking back on his life. He finally placed his mug down and traced the rim. "I'll admit, I've spent time with many women."

"Many?" The word rankled her. "Can you quantify? Does that mean a dozen? Or a hundred?"

He laughed lightly. "I like women, but believe it or not, I'm not obsessed."

"So, twelve?"

"Perhaps."

She wasn't sure why she wanted to know so badly. But a strange need drove her. "And did you love any of those twelve?"

"This sounds like a sixth question."

"It's part of number five—what have those relationships been like?"

He swished the coffee in his mug. "Most have been dalliances and nothing more."

"Most?"

"There was a woman I met in England while I was in school, but eventually I had to bring an end to our relationship."

"Why?"

"That's definitely a sixth question. And even if it's not, I'm passing on it."

"She decided you were too stubborn and arrogant?"

"Something like that." His smile didn't reach his eyes.

What had happened? Had the woman broken his heart? "And while you've been traveling? Have any other women caught your eye besides me?"

The smile turned genuine again. "No one can compare to you."

His flattery always made her stomach flutter. "Did you leave a string of broken hearts in every town you stayed in?" The question was out before she could keep herself from speaking it. But once it was, every nerve of her body perked to attention, waiting for his answer. She wanted him to answer her seriously.

He studied her face, and thankfully didn't jest. "This trip hasn't been about enjoying and spending time with women."

For a strange reason, his answer seemed to steal inside and soothe some of her angst. "I find that hard to believe about you and Declan."

"You're the first woman I've met who made me not want to leave."

His quiet statement left her suddenly breathless. She waited for him to follow up with a teasing comment or some other mirthful jab.

But he focused on his coffee mug and took a long slurp.

Did he mean what he'd said? That he didn't want to leave? Delight gently cascaded up her back.

"Time for my fifth question." He set his mug down, then swiped a piece of garlic bread left in the nearly empty basket. "Or maybe I should get six, seven, and eight too?"

"I already told you that all of my questions were related."

Even though he didn't smile this time, his eyes crinkled at the corners and were filled with warmth. "Then mine will all be related too."

"Fine."

"Why are you staying here in Fairplay?"

The question caught her off guard. From his tone, she knew he was asking her a deep question, one that had more to do with what she wanted out of life than where she lived.

"Is running this boardinghouse really what you want to do with your life?" He spoke kindly, enough that she could sense that he cared, that he wasn't asking merely to be polite.

Silently, she mulled over her responses. She wanted to be honest with him. But what could she tell him about her plans for her life when she didn't even know for herself? Yes, she'd longed for the ability to travel, see new sights, and meet new people.

But she also loved her family and couldn't abandon

their plans and hopes for a better future. "For now, I'm obligated to be here and make sure that things run smoothly."

"Until when?"

Why was he asking? "My sister Charity is planning to return in the spring, and at that point she and her husband are hoping to transform the boardinghouse into a bigger home, one that would provide a place of refuge for poor, homeless, and frightened women in need."

"And you want to help your sister with this project?"

"Of course."

One of his brows quirked. "Really?"

"Someone has to be here to manage the place until Charity gets back."

He was quiet for a moment, studying her intently.

"Fine. I love Colorado. And I love Fairplay. But I admit, I have grown restless here."

Finally, he sat back in his chair and nodded, as if she'd given him the answer he was waiting to hear.

At the sudden clatter on the front porch, she stood abruptly.

He rose too, his revolver out and pointed toward the door. His body was rigid, and his eyes narrowed, almost as if he expected someone to come barging in. He began inching toward the door and motioned toward her. "Stay back."

"Why?"

At another loud banging, he shot her a warning glare, then pressed a finger to his lips.

"What?" she whispered. "Are you worried someone is waiting to get us?"

"We have to be careful."

Careful of what? She wanted to scoff, to tell him he was overreacting, that most likely a shutter had come loose. But as he drew closer to the door, the intensity of each step told her he was afraid of something out there.

9

He should have stayed far away from Felicity. And now because of his selfishness and stupidity, he'd brought danger right to her doorstep.

"Don't come any closer," he whispered to Felicity, who was standing near the table where they'd been enjoying coffee. The remains of their meal sat in discarded piles—empty plates, silverware, serving platters, and an apple pie with a couple of slices missing.

No doubt the assassin had tracked him to the boardinghouse. A dark and stormy night would be the perfect time to show up—when he would be least expecting it.

Carefully, he turned the door handle and then began to inch it open.

A gust of frigid wind blew against it, thrusting it wide and sending a swirl of snow into the house. For a moment the snow was blowing too hard for him to see outside.

But as he stepped farther out, the light from the front window illuminated the darkness.

No one was in sight. But a tin pail had blown onto the porch—or maybe it had already been there. As another gust swept across the porch, it rattled the pail hard against the clapboards.

The sound was similar to what had disturbed them at the table. Had the noise only been the pail? Was there no one lurking outside nearby waiting to jump out and stab him?

The vision of the night he'd almost been killed rushed back.

He'd been lying in his bed trying to sleep. But he'd been restless after the argument he'd had earlier in the day with Gustaf over the rumors of unrest. His brother had been enraged to learn that Philip was growing in popularity since his return from Cambridge, so much so that people were starting to suggest he should be king instead of Gustaf. In a final parting shot, Gustaf had stopped his yelling and grown deadly calm before saying, "You will never be king. I shall make sure of that."

Philip had finally climbed out of bed to work in his darkroom—a closet he'd converted so that he had the ability to develop his photographs whenever it suited him.

Not long after he'd begun to coat the negatives with a varnish to protect their surface, he'd heard the door to his chambers creak open. With the hour having been so late, he'd been wary and had peeked out through a slit to see a man creep inside, his face masked and a dagger in hand.

It had only taken Philip a second to know what was happening—that Gustaf was carrying through on his veiled threat. Thankfully, he'd locked his darkroom door, as he often did to prevent anyone from accidentally opening it and exposing his photographs too soon.

The masked man had waited for a short while in the shadows of his bedchamber, likely intending to stab him when he exited the closet. But Philip had clattered around and whistled and acted as though he had no knowledge a murderer was lurking so close. Finally, near dawn, with the coming of light and the awakening of the servants, the assassin had left.

Philip had wasted no time in sneaking from the royal palace. He'd arranged a secret meeting with the prime minister and others of parliament who wanted to overthrow Gustaf. They'd debated for hours how to proceed. During their deliberations, they'd received news that Gustaf had learned of Philip's whereabouts and was sending a contingency of royal armed guards to arrest him on charges of treason.

Philip hadn't had any choice but to flee. And he'd been doing so ever since. He didn't know exactly how people were keeping tabs on him. There were times he suspected that the prime minister or another member of parliament had sent a bodyguard to watch him from a distance. Other times, he suspected the assassin was the one watching him and waiting to waylay him.

Whatever the case, he couldn't be too careful, especially now that he was with Felicity one more night.

He stepped onto the porch and shuddered. The temperatures had dropped drastically from earlier in the day. And from what he could tell in the light emanating onto the front yard, several inches or more of snow had fallen, covering the ice.

He made his way carefully through the dusting of snow and ice on the porch and retrieved the pail. As he turned and started back to the door, he blew out a frustrated breath at the sight of Felicity standing in the open doorway, the interior light spilling over her and revealing her in all her glorious beauty.

If an assassin was lurking in the yard somewhere with a rifle, she'd make an easy target.

"Go back in." He glowered at her as he started toward the door.

She retreated, but not before glowering back.

As he stepped inside and bolted the door behind him, he set the pail by the door, then crossed his arms. "Do you ever listen to anyone?"

"I listen to sane people instead of crazy ones who are acting as though our homestead is being attacked by a pack of hungry wolves instead of a tiny pail." She nodded at the bucket, the snow and ice melting from it and forming a puddle on the floor.

His sense of humor was gone. The moment was too grave for him to resort to his usual teasing. If only he could tell her the truth. Then she'd know why he was worried about being there. She'd know why he had to leave tomorrow.

He was like a bomb waiting to explode. And when he did, he'd hurt anyone close to him.

He rubbed his hand down his scruffy jaw and tried to expel the tension that had turned his body as rigid as ice. It didn't work. He wouldn't rest until he had the chance to go out and make sure no one was there.

He crossed the room and headed into the kitchen, where his coat and gloves and boots had been drying by the stove.

Her footsteps rushed after him. "Where are you going?"

"I'm heading out to the barn to feed the livestock." He swiped up his coat and began to stuff his arms in the sleeves, even though they were still slightly damp. "And I'll make sure everything looks okay for the night."

She reached for her coat on the peg beside the door. "I'll go with you."

His hand darted out and caught hers. This time, he met her gaze and hoped he could convey his seriousness. "Let me do this tonight for you."

She stilled and glanced at his fingers encircling hers.

"Please." He spoke the word softly. At the same time, he brushed his index finger across the back of her hand. It was a gentle but intimate caress, one he knew he had no right to.

She studied his hold a moment longer before looking up at him, her eyes filled with all kinds of emotions he wanted to explore, except that he didn't have the time. Even if he'd had time, he knew no good could come of rousing feelings between them.

But obviously his touch, even a brief one, seemed to have some effect upon her. He wasn't above utilizing it to protect her whenever necessary. Like now.

He brushed his finger down one of her fingers, then up the next, and down another, tracing them.

She inhaled softly.

He finished tracing the final two fingers before linking his pinky with hers. He wasn't playing fair, but he didn't care. "Stay here with the Kellers, and I'll be back inside soon."

The brown of her eyes had turned darker than a moonless night, inviting him to lose himself there.

Oh yes, he wanted to lose himself with Felicity Courtney, both day and night, with or without the sun or moon. But he swallowed hard, pushing the desire down. "Promise me?"

"Fine." The word was short, as though she could barely get it out.

He pulled his hand away from hers and finished bundling up.

She watched him as though she was imagining his touch all over again. And as he tugged on his boots and hat and gloves, he could feel her eyes on him as if they were her hands. When he exited with a lantern in hand, he didn't dodge the blowing snow that slapped at him. Instead, he lifted his face into the wind and took the punishment for grazing her fingers so intimately.

Already the attraction between him and Felicity was strong. And he couldn't add to it and make her harder to resist. He had to remain a gentleman and keep proper boundaries at all times. No more gentle grazing of her hand, even in an emergency.

The lantern light sputtered in the wind and went out almost immediately, and darkness closed in all around. The ground was still slick with ice underneath the layer of snow. The wind slithered beneath his coat and sent chills over his skin, froze his cheeks and nose and prickled his fingers—reminding him of how close he'd come to freezing earlier in the day.

After trudging forward against the blowing wind for what felt like much too long, a nagging fear crept in. Had he overshot the barn? Was he wandering the wrong direction altogether?

He darted a look over his shoulder and glimpsed the faint light emanating from the house. Then he forced himself to keep going. Next time, he'd bring a rope with him and attach it to the house and barn so that, after he left, Felicity would have a way to guide herself during any more storms. He'd heard tales of how much snow fell at times in the high country. And he didn't want her getting lost in the dark and wandering around, unable to return to the house.

Finally he bumped into a post, which he guessed was part of the goat pen. He used the fence to guide himself to the barn door, and then once inside, he relit the lantern.

The cats and goats and chickens and even the lone gelding greeted him, obviously relieved to see him. He gave them all plenty of feed. The water troughs were full, and even though it was cold outside, the barn had retained some warmth from all the creatures huddled inside.

After scouring the corners of the barn and as much of the surrounding area as he could without the lantern blowing out, he tried to reassure himself that no one was there, that he was fine for one more night. Then he located a couple of ropes and tied them together before fastening one end to the barn and starting back to the house.

The wind and snow wrestled against him, as if to keep him away from Felicity. But he pressed forward, the glow from the windows guiding him back. When he reached the cellar, he ran out of rope and had to tie the end to the cellar door. But thankfully, the back entrance to the house was only a dozen paces away, and he used the side of the house to guide him there.

As he pushed the door open and stumbled inside, Felicity was wiping her hands on a rag, the dinner dishes mostly washed, only a pan left in the sink.

He was covered in a layer of snow and half frozen—not nearly as cold as earlier, but stiff nonetheless.

She reached for the top button of his coat. "How was the pack of wolves waiting to tear down our house?"

"They're vicious. I fought them away with my bare hands." He tried for a smile.

She cocked her head as though she could see through his humor. "Then I guess you deserve another cup of coffee and a second slice of pie for your bravery."

"Why, yes, actually I do. I'm glad you agree." The banter came easily again. And it was a safer place for their conversation—a place where they wouldn't have to worry about growing too close.

Her fingers flew down his coat, and before he knew it, she was tugging him free, shaking off the layer of snow. Within minutes, he disposed of his outer garb, had a cup of coffee to warm his hands, and was eating a second piece of pie.

He stood at the center worktable and savored the moment as she finished cleaning up their supper. He purposefully kept the conversation lighter. As she wiped down the sauce splatters on the stove, he tucked away his last bite and washed it down with the coffee.

If only he could have many more such evenings in his life, he'd die a happy man. Even as the thought came, he rapidly banished it. "I know what you're scheming."

"You do?" One of her brows rose.

"Yes, you tempted me this morning with the scent of the sauce and the bread, giving me no choice but to come back for the meal tonight."

"Oh, so you battled the ice and the freezing rain so that you could taste my cooking?"

"Exactly."

"You told me you came because you couldn't force yourself to leave Fairplay without seeing me one more time. But all along, you came for the food."

"I did." He used his finger to get a last dollop of the cinnamon sauce left on his plate. As he stuck his finger in his mouth, she paused in polishing the iron stovetop to watch him. He had a sudden need to go slow and make a show of licking all his fingers and gauging her reaction as he did so. But he refrained.

Even so, as he finished cleaning off his finger, her eyes grew wide and a flush moved into her cheeks. For all of her wit and the attention she garnered from men, she was clearly an innocent. And that thought pleased him more than it should.

"With the storm outside, it's a good thing you have a big, strong man around."

"A big, strong man?" She scanned the room with faux innocence. "Where?"

He chuckled. "Just admit it. You're glad I'm here." He resisted the urge to swipe his finger across the pie plate again, and instead, set the dish on the worktable.

"And why should I be glad?"

"I can chop wood for you."

She gathered up a couple of misshapen pieces from the wood bin. "I hate to be the one to inform you, but my five-year-old self could chop wood better than this."

"You're brutal." He laid a hand over his heart, feigning a wound.

She dropped the logs back onto the pile he'd cut that morning. Then she brushed the dust and wood chips from her hand. "I'll admit, your strangely cut pieces are better than nothing."

"Is that your way of thanking me for replenishing the wood box?" With the way the storm was raging outside, he was glad he'd taken the time to bring in the fuel before it became drenched with rain and ice.

"It might be."

"If it isn't, I know another way you can thank me." The flirtatious words were out before he could stop them.

In the process of draping a damp towel over the edge of the sink, she paused. For several irregular beats of his heart, the howl of the wind and the rattle of the house echoed in the kitchen.

He was tempted to grin and tap at his lips so that she knew exactly what kind of thank-you he wanted. But again, he forced himself to swallow his desire for her and instead kept the conversation from getting too intimate.

"Don't you want to know how?" he persisted.

"No." Her expression turned adorably sassy. "I can already guess what you have in mind."

"You can?"

"Yes, because you're a shameless ladies' man."

"I thought we already determined at dinner that I'm not interested in anyone else but you." His words came out light and teasing, and he hoped his tone masked just how interested he was in her. In fact, his interest was growing larger and more life-sized every moment he was with her.

"I'm the apple pie of the day." Her retort was tart. "I'm sure you'll find a new favorite flavor soon enough."

"I can't imagine ever getting tired of apple pie." This time his comment came out low and full of suggestion, and the second it did, he wanted to palm his forehead.

She just shook her head, her lips pursed even as the flush remained in her cheeks.

He made himself smile casually, but deep in his gut, heat was smoldering.

At a soft thump overhead, he forced his gaze to the

ceiling. "I think it's time for Mrs. Keller to have a break. I'll go sit with Mr. Keller for a while."

"I can do it."

He started toward the door that led into the front sitting room. "Let me give the two of you one more night's break."

She didn't respond right away, but her footsteps followed after him. Was she thinking about how they were in the same position as the previous night? That their time together was short? That all too soon, she'd be back to having disrupted sleep at night?

At the bottom of the steps, he paused and looked back at her. She stood in the kitchen door, the lantern glow outlining her, making her look like an angel radiating heavenly light. The overwhelming urge prodded him to go back and gently brush his lips to hers. A tiny kiss. Soft, short, and sweet. That was all.

No. He couldn't. Not now. And not anytime.

Even if someday he could wrestle himself free of Gustaf's threats, would she be someone parliament would consider for his wife? A young, beautiful American without any prominent family ties, no political influence, and no impressive lineage. She had some wealth, but certainly nothing that would make her an advantageous match in the eyes of those who would be deciding for him.

He couldn't let himself fall for her. And he certainly

couldn't give her reason to fall for him.

"Get a good night's sleep. Please." Then without waiting for her response, he hurried up the stairs before he changed his mind and went back to her.

10

The howling of the wind woke Felicity. And the frigidness of the air.

She burrowed under the heavy layer of blankets covering her, not wanting to face the coldness. For a moment, she hovered between waking and sleeping, but at the clank of the stove door in the kitchen, she sat up.

Darkness permeated the room. Was it nearing dawn?

She gathered up the mound of blankets and draped them around her. Then she perched on the edge of her bed and searched for her bedroom slippers. She stuffed her feet in, the chill already turning her toes to ice.

She dragged herself and the covers up, threw open her door, and startled at the sight of a dark outline in front of the stove. The embers inside illuminated a man's body. Philip's.

"Good morning." His voice rumbled low.

The sound of it did strange things to her insides,

fanning heat and sending warmth to her limbs and cheeks. Thankfully, it didn't cause the same reaction she'd had to him last night when he'd grazed her hand, when she'd become almost incoherent in the midst of the sensations he'd awakened inside her.

"Good morning." Her reply came out husky and embarrassed her even more.

"How did you sleep?" He added wood shavings and bark to the embers.

"I didn't wake up once."

"Good." He used the poker to stir the embers so that the newest chips would catch fire.

"How about you? Did you get any sleep?"

"A night or two without sleep won't hurt me." Philip straightened and studied her. Though she couldn't see his expression, she could feel him taking in her tousled hair, the hem of her nightgown showing beneath the blankets, her bare ankles, and the slippers.

She felt suddenly breathless and tugged the blankets around her more securely. "So you stayed up all night?"

"It went fast. I enjoyed reading to Mr. Keller."

"He's a sweet man." Philip sitting beside Mr. Keller's bed all night was one of the kindest and noblest things she'd ever known a man to do. Not many men—or women—would be willing to make such a sacrifice for a stranger.

The wind took that moment to rattle the

windowpanes as if it intended to shake them loose altogether. A whistle of wind also blew through the stovepipe, the cold air almost dousing the flames.

Philip grabbed another handful of fuel and began to layer the pieces carefully over the fire. He had on his coat—likely to ward off the chill—but underneath, his shirt was untucked in the front, some of the top buttons undone, and one of his suspenders dangled by his trousers.

The glow of the kindling revealed the stubble on his jaw, darker and thicker than yesterday. His hair fell forward, practically hanging in his eyes. And his lips were set in a stubborn line, as if he were daring the wind to defy his efforts to keep the fire going.

He looked so good she just wanted to stand there all day and stare at him. Maybe she would . . .

He smirked at her over his shoulder, clearly sensing her appraisal or fascination or both.

Ugh. She gave herself a mental shake. She had to keep her feelings under control. She was a strong woman and didn't need a man in her life. She had to keep reminding herself of that.

Besides, he had to be tired and deserved to rest, not do all the chores—not after being up all night. She started toward him. "Here. Let me take care of starting the fire. You go lie down and sleep."

He didn't budge from where he was layering the

sticks. "Sounds like you're concerned about me."

"No more or less concerned than I would be with any other guest." She reached his side and then picked up a larger limb from the wood box.

"Admit you're worried about me taxing myself."

She added her log to the now crackling flames and stood beside him, basking in the warmth of the growing fire.

He bumped her arm with his playfully. "Go ahead."

"Fine. You've been so decent and kind that I don't want you to feel obligated to do any more than you already have." In the darkness of predawn in the cozy glow of the stove, it was all too easy to spill the truth.

He stood silently, as if her sincerity had taken him off guard. "I don't feel obligated in the least, Felicity. I'm honestly quite relieved I'm here to assist you." His words held sincerity too.

She liked his humor, his wit, and his playfulness. But she liked when he was serious too, like now. She could sense his shift and wanted to hang on to the moment for as long as possible. How could she do that except by letting down her guard and being serious in return? "I admit I'm relieved you're here too. I appreciate your help."

He focused on the flames. "I wish there was a way that we could hire a nurse to help the Kellers."

"A nurse?"

"Or at least someone who can provide care and perhaps even has ideas for how to make the quality of his life better."

Her mind began to whirl at the possibilities. It really was a good idea and would benefit the Kellers. But would her sisters allow her to spend their money on such an endeavor? And even if they did, would she be able to find a nurse who would be willing to move to Fairplay and live at the boardinghouse?

"While I'm in Denver," he said quietly, as though reading her mind, "I can make some inquiries."

Yes, he was leaving. She didn't need the reminder. And yet, she couldn't fault him for bringing it up. He was only being kind to make such an offer. "Do you think we really could find someone?"

"I shall surely try." He reached for another log and added it to the flames.

"Thank you, Philip."

He straightened, then nudged her arm with his again. "If you continue calling me Philip, I might keep doing nice things for you."

"If that's all it takes to have you at my beck and call, then I'll definitely agree to it."

"You have me at your beck and call even if you do nothing at all."

"That's good to know." Even though his tone hinted at playfulness, it also contained the same sincerity as before, and it melted her heart just a little bit more.

"In fact, I'm going out right now to check on the animals—"

"You can't."

"I've done so previously, and you found no fault with my work, did you?"

"I'm not questioning your ability. I'm insisting that you go to bed and let me handle the livestock."

"No." His tone turned hard and stubborn the same way it had last night when he'd so valiantly defended them from the pail on the porch.

"I've been doing it every day since Patience moved out. And I'll continue long after you're gone."

"Hopefully Weston can ride over later today to check on you and help with the evening chores." Philip rubbed his hands together in front of the flames.

Was this a purposeful name drop—similar to his mention of Denver—to again remind her of his imminent departure?

If so, it was working.

As Philip prepared to go outside, she twisted free a scarf from the peg near the kitchen door. As she extended it to him, he leaned down and waited, his slow smile giving her silent permission to wrap it around his neck for herself.

She hesitated. Doing so seemed like such a wifelike task. But now that she'd offered, she couldn't take the scarf back, could she?

Avoiding his lively gaze, she tossed the scarf first one way around his neck and then the other, doing her best not to touch him, although her fingers twitched with the need to comb through his hair.

As she finished, she hugged the blankets to her body again.

"I suppose now you'll want to kiss my cheek?" He held his face out sideways, giving her full access to his cheek.

"With all the hair growing there, I'd rather kiss a cactus." That wasn't true. She imagined the scruff was bristly and rough to the touch, but for some reason the prospect of letting her fingers glide over all that bristly roughness sent a tremor through her belly.

"I guarantee that once you get a taste of me, you won't go back to kissing anything or anyone else ever again." With that, he winked at her.

She just shook her head, even as a flush spread through her. She'd actually only kissed one suitor before. On the very same night he'd rejected her and left her sitting alone in the drawing room of her friend's house in Pennsylvania. She'd thought he'd cared for her. But she'd simply been a pretty face and an easy conquest. And the young ladies she'd believed were her friends had been waiting in the hallway, laughing at her for how gullible she'd been.

She'd never let any other suitor kiss her since. In fact, she'd resolved she wouldn't let another man kiss her unless he made a commitment to marry her. Even then, she guessed she wouldn't really be ready to kiss anyone until she had a ring on her finger and the reverend declared them man and wife.

Thankfully, Philip was already on his way to the door and hadn't stopped to analyze her reaction to his playful request. He had to yank for several hard pulls before the door finally opened, then only by inches, but it was enough that a shower of snow blew inside.

The drift against the door tumbled down onto the kitchen floor. Though darkness still hovered over the yard, it was easy to see that the snow was still falling heavily and that many inches had accumulated overnight.

The trip to the barn would be difficult in the blowing and drifting, especially with so much to wade through. "Maybe you should wait until morning light to venture out?"

The moment he stepped outside, the wind snuffed out the light in his lantern.

"Philip, wait." She moved into the doorway, cold, dry snow swirling against her, attempting to wrest the blankets from her grip.

Only a foot from the door, he stopped. "You can't resist kissing my cheek after all?"

"It's going to be difficult to find the barn." He could

very well get lost if the snow and darkness pushed him off course. That very thing had almost happened to Patience last winter. Thankfully, her sister had the wherewithal to turn around and come back to the house. "The animals can survive a while longer without attention."

Philip nodded ahead. "I fastened a rope last night, one that leads from the house out to the barn. I'll be alright."

She peered into the darkness, searching for the line. She didn't see anything, and as he disappeared into a cloud of blowing snow, she could only pray he'd make it there quickly, without any mishaps.

She closed the door, and as she swept up the snow, she couldn't keep a bubble of hope from rising inside. What if the weather remained too stormy today for Philip to depart? What if he had to stay another whole day? Or what if he was trapped in the high country all winter?

It was only the end of October, too soon for winter to settle in fully. The weather would warm up enough to melt the snow in and around Fairplay. But what about in the higher elevations? In the mountain passes? Would those be closed now due to the treacherous conditions?

As she started making breakfast—eggs, bacon, and flap jacks—she couldn't keep her mind from spinning with the possibility of him living at the boardinghouse and taking the job as the hired hand.

Some people might not think such a living arrangement was proper, since she was a single woman and he was a single man. But the Kellers were there as chaperones, weren't they?

As the light of dawn began to show through the blowing and drifting snow, she took breakfast and broth up to the Kellers. Their woodbin was beginning to run low, so she filled it, taking from the woodbins in the kitchen and front room. Even then, the room upstairs had turned frigid—likely from how hard the wind was still blowing.

If the storm continued for much longer, she would have to consider moving Mr. Keller downstairs into the front room, perhaps having him sleep on the sofa temporarily.

Daylight continued to break, but Philip didn't return.

Felicity began pacing the length of the kitchen, stopping every minute or so to scrape away the ice on the window and peer out toward the barn only to see more of the blowing and swirling white.

After what seemed hours, her pulse was beating too thunderously for her to sit back and wait any longer. She bundled up in her coat and hat. She'd just started pulling on her boots when the kitchen door slammed open and Philip stepped inside, his arms loaded with wood.

He'd covered his face with her scarf so only his eyes were showing. His eyebrows were coated in snow and ice, and his coat and clothing were covered too. He dumped the wood, then began to back out of the door, as if he intended to return into the storm. His gaze snagged on her, and he stopped.

For a moment, he fumbled to close the door, kicking the wood out of the way and pushing against the force of the wind. When he had it shut finally, he spun, yanked down the scarf, and scowled at her. "Where do you think you're going?"

"You've been gone so long I thought you'd gotten lost."

"Did you stop to think that if I was lost, you might not be able to find me and that you'd end up lost too?" His voice was testy.

"Did you stop to think that if something happened to you out there, I wouldn't be able to sit in here and do nothing?"

He pinned her with his blue eyes, which had turned from the usual light and playful shade to dark and serious. "I'm fine, Felicity. I had to break the ice on the trough. And then I chopped more wood."

"How was I to know that?"

"You have to trust me."

"But—"

"We have mountains with snow and blizzards in my country too, you know." He shed one of his gloves.

"But don't you have servants who take care of you?"

"I can take care of myself." He took a step closer. Before she knew what he was doing, he lifted his hand to her cheek and drew a gentle line along her jaw.

Her breath snagged sharply in her chest. The touch was as light as a dusting of sugar sprinkles, but it sent enormous waves of awareness to every part of her body. Her instant reaction to him was as intense as it had been last night when he'd grazed each of her fingers so languidly. It seemed to melt her insides, like low heat melting butter and drizzling it around her body.

The deliciousness only made her want another caress, made her want more of something she couldn't name.

His fingertips lingered at the edge of her jaw. And his gaze had followed, as delicate but searing as his touch. "Promise you'll stay here inside the house and not come out?" His voice was so soft and pleading that she wouldn't have been able to resist him even if she'd wanted to—which she didn't.

She nodded.

"Say it." He tucked a strand of her hair behind her ear.

She closed her eyes at the sweet heat of the touch.

"Promise me."

"I promise." She wasn't sure exactly what he was asking of her, but with his fingers upon her, she couldn't think, couldn't resist, couldn't do anything except what he asked.

He let his hand fall away and took a step back.

Her eyes flew open to find him tugging on his glove

and readying to go back out. As he opened the door, he nodded at her. "I'll be back with more wood shortly."

She couldn't think of a response. Instead, she watched mutely as he closed the door behind himself and disappeared.

Once he was gone, she sagged against the center worktable. All along, she'd been able to admit he was a good-looking man. She hadn't wanted to like him, hadn't wanted to become one more woman—among a string of many—to walk in and out of his life. So she'd tried hard to keep from allowing any attraction to spring to life inside her.

How was it that within just two days and a couple of innocent touches, the attraction had not only sprung up but had developed into a full-grown living and breathing force?

Maybe it would have been better for Philip to leave yesterday after all. Or even today. Because she wasn't sure how her heart would be able to resist him or even if she wanted to try.

11

He wasn't leaving today. That much was certain.

Philip peered through the spot he'd scraped in the frosted front window. Beyond the porch, the wind continued to gust, causing drifts as high as several feet in some places. Not only that, but the blowing snow was so thick that when he'd been out in it earlier in the day, he'd hardly been able to see his hand outstretched in front of him, clinging to the rope that led back from the barn.

"Looks like you're officially stuck with me one more night." He let the lacy curtain fall and turned to face Felicity where she sat in a chair beside Mr. Keller, who was lying on the sofa. Mrs. Keller reclined in the other wingback chair, her crochet hook weaving up and down through her colorful pattern of yarn.

They'd decided to bring the Kellers down into the front room since the upstairs had become so cold that the water in the wash basin had frozen over.

In spite of the chill, Philip had slept for the past several hours upstairs in one of the rooms. But even with a heavy layer of blankets, the frigidness had finally awoken him and driven him out of bed.

Now crowded together in the front room and with the stove pumping out heat, they were staying warm enough. At least for the short term.

He hadn't wanted to worry Felicity, but there weren't many dry logs stacked under the lean-to by the barn. That morning, he'd chopped at least half of what was there and brought it inside. But with how cold it was, they'd been using the fuel faster than expected, which was partly why he'd supported bringing the Kellers downstairs for the duration of the storm. Then they would only need to keep two stoves fueled—the front room and kitchen—rather than three.

He guessed they had enough to keep them fueled through the end of the day, but not for the coming night. At some point, he was going to have to head out and actually cut down a tree. Or perhaps find windfall and drag it back to the lean-to. Hopefully he'd be able to find something that wasn't saturated from all the rain and ice that had fallen before changing to snow.

"You are rather hard to put up with." Felicity shot a glance his way while holding Mr. Keller's hand between both of hers, blowing on it once in a while as if to warm it.

After the past night of staying awake and listening to Philip read, Mr. Keller had dozed most of the day. But at the moment, his eyes were open and as knowing as always. They communicated, as they had all along, that Mr. Keller knew who he was—a prince of Lapland and part of the royal lineage.

Thankfully, the older man couldn't divulge that information to anyone.

As Felicity squeezed Mr. Keller's hand, the older man seemed to try to squeeze her hand in return. But nothing about his body worked from his shoulders down to his toes. And although he'd lost function of some of his muscles in his face, at least he still had the ability to intake liquids.

"But I suppose we can try to endure one more night with you," Felicity offered.

Mrs. Keller paused in her crocheting and glanced overhead, the wind still rattling the house as if it might tear it apart. "It might be more than one more night."

That was what he was afraid of.

As if hearing his thoughts, Felicity cast him a sideways glance. "With all the snow, what will you do if you can't get out of the high country until spring?"

"Guess I'll have to stay and get married." He kept his tone light and teasing, but even as he said the words, something inside him flared at the prospect of doing that very thing with Felicity. He never would. It was entirely implausible. But still . . . a part of him wished he were free to live the way he wanted without worrying about the repercussions.

Felicity was shaking her head. "I don't know if Mrs. Bancroft would accept your proposal. But maybe if you increase your charm, you'll eventually convince her."

He grinned. "I think we both know there isn't any amount of charm in the world that could make her into a nicer person."

"You're right. She'll most certainly reject you and devastate you. You'd be safer to remain single."

"Safer single?" He lifted his brows. "Hibernating alone might be safer, but it's certainly not as pleasurable as having a beautiful woman with me."

She ducked her head and fidgeted with Mr. Keller's blanket, her cheeks flushing.

Mr. and Mrs. Keller were now both watching him, their eyes alight with interest, as if he were performing a rendition of a Beethoven symphony.

He supposed the banter with Felicity was entertaining. At least, it was to him.

But what if she was right? What if he was in the high country until spring? The thought had pinged around his head already over the course of the afternoon, leaving him with an ache in his temples. If he had no way to get out, would that mean an assassin would have no way to get in? That was assuming the assassin wasn't already somewhere in the area, holed up and waiting for the blizzard to pass.

After scouring the barn and other outbuildings again this morning, he'd seen no evidence that anyone else was near the homestead. As long as the blizzard lasted and the snow made traveling difficult, they were safe. He could breathe easier and let himself relax a little. And perhaps he could permit himself to enjoy the extra day or two he would get to spend with Felicity.

Could he throw away caution for now and simply relish the present?

He wanted to try. If he really was getting a much-needed reprieve from his brother's threats, why not make the most of the time?

With a new sense of resolve, he crossed to his camera box where Felicity had placed it next to the sideboard. "I have the perfect way for us to pass the afternoon."

He flipped open the lid of the case and lifted out the bulky camera. He kicked the legs open on the tripod and situated the camera at the center, positioning it so that the lens was pointed at Felicity.

She was watching him and was as absolutely stunning as always with her eyes wide and framed by her long lashes and her lips parted as though she intended to trade more quips with him. He wanted to keep the lens on her and memorize every curve and line and freckle on her face.

But he stepped away from his camera so that he didn't

do something to humiliate himself, like walk over to her, draw her up into his arms, and start placing kisses all over her face. "We'll turn the sitting room into a studio, and I'll take photographs of everyone."

Her lips quirked knowingly. "So that you have my picture to take with you when you leave?"

"Of course I want your picture. But you have to know I won't need it to remember you, since you are unforgettable."

Mrs. Keller smiled at his compliment, as if he'd paid it to her instead of Felicity. And although Felicity didn't respond, her lips curled up into a fuller smile.

"Now, ladies." He waved his hand with a flourish. "Go don your very best gowns and prepare yourself for the finest portrait you'll ever have taken."

They both stood in a flutter of excitement, and Mrs. Keller patted her hair. "I haven't had a photograph taken since our wedding day."

Felicity brushed a few strands of her hair back too. "I haven't ever had a photograph."

In the process of securing the camera to the tripod, Philip straightened. "Never one?"

"Never one."

"Then we must most certainly rectify that today. I shall take a dozen of you."

She laughed lightly, the sound tinged with delight. "I'm sure one will be sufficient."

"Not for me." He didn't bother to hide his desire but let it rumble into his voice.

She just shook her head and started toward her bedroom off the kitchen.

Mrs. Keller hesitated at the bottom of the steps.

He offered her a smile. "I'll watch Mr. Keller while you take your time getting pretty."

"Thank you, Philip." She started up the first step, then stopped and glanced over her shoulder at him. "Mr. Keller was always generous with his compliments toward me the way you are with Felicity."

Their gazes shifted to the older man on the sofa, his eyes closed, his expression peaceful in sleep. "I can tell he still loves you by the way he looks at you."

She nodded and dropped her gaze shyly. "Don't ever stop telling Felicity how much she means to you. Do it every day for her whole life, as much as you're able."

He could only watch in silence as Mrs. Keller raced up the stairway. He didn't have the heart to tell her that he wouldn't be in Felicity's future, that he didn't even have a right to compliment her in the present.

So why was he paying attention to her and flirting as if there were no tomorrow? Why wasn't he taking more care with his words? And his touch? He'd grazed her cheek this morning to stop her from going outside. After touching her fingers last night, he'd told himself he wouldn't use the power of their attraction to his advantage. But it was so hard to refrain . . .

Since their first meeting, their banter had been harmless and in good fun—at least on his part. But over the past couple of days, something had shifted and become more serious, and he wasn't sure why. Maybe it was because she'd collapsed in front of his eyes. Maybe it was because he'd learned just how deeply caring she was to sacrifice her health for the Kellers. Maybe it was because the storm had forced them into proximity. Maybe it was because they'd gotten to know each other in a way they hadn't been able to do at any of Mrs. Bancroft's dinner parties.

Whatever it was, he didn't want to lead her to believe they could have a relationship, only to end up hurting her. Yes, she was a strong woman and didn't take him too seriously most of the time. But surely she was feeling everything he was, if he was reading her correctly—and he was fairly confident that he was.

He rested his head against his camera, the war inside him raging. He should have left Fairplay several weeks ago when he'd originally planned—shouldn't have allowed himself to stay. But he'd been too enamored with her and too weak to tear himself away. And he still couldn't.

He lifted his head and glanced toward the door and the layer of snow that had blown underneath and was now crusted to the floor. He couldn't go anywhere, not anytime soon. And the honest truth—the deep, gut-wrenching truth: now that he was here with her, he was not only relieved to be by her side during this dangerous storm, but he didn't want to be anywhere else.

All the while he finished setting up his camera and the dry plate, he strengthened his resolve to treat Felicity as a friend and nothing more. When Mrs. Keller returned in a lovely gown, they tended to Mr. Keller, suctioning his mouth and repositioning him. All the while, the older man's eyes never once left his wife and were filled with both love and adoration.

As Philip helped to situate Mrs. Keller in a chair, he couldn't keep from noticing how she seemed to grow more beautiful under her husband's admiration, almost as if he were the fertilizer and water and sunshine that she needed.

Philip focused the lens, slipped in the dry plate, then draped the black cloth over his head. As he readied to take Mrs. Keller's picture, he could sense Felicity's presence before he heard her footsteps. He had the urge to pull out from underneath the dark linen. But he held himself steady and forced himself to pay attention to Mrs. Keller.

Only after he'd made sure he had a perfect shot of her did he flip the cloth up and emerge. He couldn't keep himself from seeking out Felicity before he looked anywhere else.

She stood just inside the door.

At the sight of her, his jaw dropped open.

He'd seen her in her fanciest gowns during the dinners at Mrs. Bancroft's, but she'd never worn this particular one. It was a dark purple with a narrow fit that showed off her curves to perfection. The bustle on the back highlighted her womanly figure too, as did the sleekness of the bodice.

She'd piled her hair into a fashionable twist at the top of her head, which left her graceful neck entirely exposed. Adorned by a simple gold necklace and delicate gold earrings, she had an understated elegance.

She held herself with poise, and yet, from the slight tilt of her head, she seemed to be waiting for him to comment on her appearance.

But what could he say that wouldn't turn him into a milksop? He certainly couldn't tell her how he really felt—that she was the most ravishing woman he'd ever met and that he wanted to stare at her all day, all night, and forever.

"It's too much, isn't it?" She finally spoke, her tone edged with embarrassment.

He managed to close his mouth. "You're perfect." The words came out with so much awe that he should have been embarrassed himself except that he was rarely embarrassed about anything.

She offered him a small smile.

He needed to see that smile grow large, wanted to give her something to smile about all the time. "You're so perfect you will probably break the camera with how pretty you are."

Yes, he was turning into a milksop. But he didn't care, because her smile widened, just the way he'd hoped.

Mrs. Keller was standing beside her husband and was holding his hand as she wiped liquid from his chin. "She looks like a princess."

Mr. Keller's eyes brightened, as if his wife had voiced his sentiments.

Princess? Philip took her in again, this time more objectively, seeing her the way the people of Lapland would. He could envision her sitting down to dinner with his family and friends at the long, polished table set to perfection. He could picture her dancing with him in the ballroom, her lush brown eyes only on him. He could imagine strolling together in the gardens outside the ballroom with her arm tucked into his. And he could definitely visualize bending down and kissing her in the moonlight.

Everyone would likely agree with Mr. and Mrs. Keller's assessment, that Felicity indeed looked the part of a princess. But would having the bearing and appearance of royalty be enough? Or would everyone condemn her for being a commoner and a foreigner?

And would it really matter what anyone thought? If Gustaf remained king, Philip might never be able to return to Lapland. He might have to keep his secret identity and live in obscurity for the rest of his life. Could he do that here? With her?

He approached her, bowed formally, then held out his arm. "May I, my lady?"

The smile that was on her lips finally reached her eyes. "Yes, you may, my lord."

Your Highness. That was the proper form of address for a prince. But he hadn't heard it in over a year. Only from Declan once in a while when they were in private.

Not that he wanted Felicity to use his royal address. But he had the sudden strange longing for her to know about the real him and not this pretend version that he'd had to project.

But what was the point in telling her? What would it accomplish? He'd only risk her treating him differently— or at least viewing him differently. He didn't want her bowing and deferring and hallowing him the way most subjects in his country did. In fact, he'd rather liked the casual way he'd been able to interact with average people—something that never happened in Lapland.

Knowing Felicity as he did, he doubted a revelation of his being a prince would change how she treated him. She was authentic, and from what he'd witnessed of her during her time at Mrs. Bancroft's, she didn't treat people differently based on their wealth and status or lack thereof. She was respectful and kind to all.

He finished escorting her with the pomp that came

easily from years of practice, then he helped to seat her. While he readied a new plate, she fidgeted with her skirt and repositioned herself first one way, then another, asking Mrs. Keller for advice on what looked the best.

As the lens focused in on her face, he let himself simply stare at her, taking in every minute detail from the sweeping arch of her eyebrows and the high smooth cheekbone to the curl caressing her cheek—just the way his fingers itched to do.

Only when she stared directly at the lens and quirked a brow did he realize he'd been pressed against his camera for an abnormally long time.

He pulled back and straightened, trying to appear nonchalant.

But Mrs. Keller was watching him with an amused expression, as though she was beginning to understand just how obsessed he was with Felicity.

"You will be stunning any way you sit." He pretended to adjust the bellows. Maybe taking photographs of her hadn't been his best idea. He was already having a difficult time keeping his eyes and thoughts in line concerning Felicity. And staring at her through his camera lens wasn't helping matters.

But he couldn't stop now. Even if she was unforgettable, he wanted the photographs to take back with him. In fact, he desperately wanted them. He didn't care that pictures of a beautiful American woman wouldn't be appropriate to keep around, especially once he was engaged. He didn't care that if anyone saw the prints, they'd assume less than noble reasons for his having them.

The truth was growing clearer with every passing moment—he couldn't imagine himself with any woman other than Felicity. But the other truth was that he couldn't imagine how he'd be able to have a life with her. Not without subjecting her to danger or disapproval. Or both.

12

Felicity couldn't stop shivering. A draft circled around her pallet and under her blanket and coat. In addition, the floorboards themselves had cold rising through the cracks so that she couldn't get comfortable.

Her gaze darted to the sofa and the stack of blankets piled over Mr. Keller. They'd covered him with almost every blanket in the house. It was already difficult enough to keep him warm, but with the shortage of dry wood, the situation was growing dire.

And while Felicity didn't begrudge the dear man one single blanket, she hadn't been able to sleep much, especially as the temperature dropped dangerously low. She didn't have a thermometer to know exactly how cold it was outside, but the water remaining in the sink in the kitchen had frozen, as had the water in the washbasin beside the back door.

If they'd been able to fuel the kitchen stove, the extra

warmth would have driven off some of the chill. But during the last hours of daylight, Philip had braved the blizzard to seek out more wood. He'd even managed to chop a tree near the edge of the yard and had dragged it into the barn to cut into smaller usable pieces only to find that it was too wet to be of any use. It had only smoked and sizzled without providing much-needed heat.

They'd made the decision to conserve the few logs they had left. To do so, they'd agreed to congregate in the front room for the night and use only the stove there.

The flame in the lantern on the sofa table gave Mrs. Keller enough light to monitor her husband's condition, but it didn't disturb Felicity as she tried to sleep.

If only she could sleep . . .

Not only was the shivering preventing her slumber, but she was worried about Philip, who'd gone out again to scavenge for more wood.

She prayed he'd be able to find some that hadn't been drenched and frozen. If he didn't, she wasn't sure what they would do. Start burning furniture?

At the moment, she was half-tempted to sit up and toss in the little stool that sat in front of one of the wingback chairs. But how long would they derive warmth from a meager stool before the frigidness of the night crept back in?

Felicity pushed up to her elbow. "You're sure you don't want me to sit with Mr. Keller while you rest?"

Mrs. Keller huddled beneath layers of clothing and blankets too. "I'm wide awake, dear. You try to sleep."

Felicity laid her head back down on her pillow, but at the rattle of the back door, she scrambled to her feet. Finally, Philip was back.

Her pulse rolled forward like the wheels of a train, chugging slowly but picking up speed. She pattered in her several pairs of stockings toward the kitchen door, dragging her blanket with her.

The whoosh of the arctic air greeted her first. The normally warm kitchen was frozen, and more so with the open door. Philip was dumping what appeared to be cut wood into the bin beside the stove.

"You found wood?" She shuddered down to her bones even as she made her way into the kitchen toward him.

He shoved the door closed and then dropped a second armful of wood onto the floor. He was wearing her scarf again, tugged up over his nose. The hat on his head was pulled low, so that only his eyes showed.

He dragged the scarf away from his mouth. "I chopped up the extra stall in the barn."

She hated that they'd had to resort to the destruction. But what choice did they have if they didn't want to freeze to death? "That was smart. Much better than burning the furniture, which was what I was seriously contemplating."

"Then you don't mind?"

"Without more heat, I'm afraid Mr. Keller may not survive the night." She whispered her fear, praying Mrs. Keller couldn't hear her morbid prediction.

Philip nodded and then began to fumble at his coat, his fingers clearly stiff and frozen.

She crossed to him and pushed his hand out of the way and began to assist him. Even though the kitchen was unlit, the glow from the other room provided enough light that she could find his snow-covered buttons.

"I had to shovel at least three feet of snow away from the barn door before I could open it." His body radiated cold that only made her shiver all the more.

"Will the livestock make it?"

"They seem to be okay." His warm whisper bathed her forehead. "I think the drifts of snow are insulating at least one wall of the barn, where most of them have gathered."

"Good." Even so, she wouldn't be surprised if some of the animals—the weakest or youngest—didn't make it.

Her own fingers were stiffening with each button she touched on his frozen coat.

But he waited patiently for her help, almost as if he'd run out of energy to help himself. She could only guess how exhausted he was. After sitting the previous two nights at Mr. Keller's bedside and only getting a few hours of sleep during the day, and now having spent part of the night chopping fuel in the barn, he would grow ill if he wasn't more careful. She ought to know.

"I'm sorry for all that you're having to do." She slipped open the last button and started to tug off a sleeve.

"Don't be sorry." Weariness etched his voice, leaving no room for his usual teasing.

As a matter of fact, he'd been more serious since the photography session that afternoon.

Warmth puddled in her stomach at the remembrance of how he'd stared at her during the picture-taking. From the moment she'd stepped into the room until she'd exited again after they'd finished, he'd hardly taken his eyes from her. Even when he'd been under the black cloth and looking through his camera lens, his attention had been intense, so much that her skin felt as though it were burning, and she'd almost gone after her smelling salts except that she hadn't been sure she'd be able to cross the room without fainting.

He'd taken a dozen pictures of her in a variety of poses—some sitting, some standing, some smiling, some serious. He'd even convinced her to uncoil her hair for the last two pictures and let it hang down.

At the end of the session, he'd stepped out onto the front porch. She hadn't needed Mrs. Keller to smile and tell her that Philip was overheated because of her. The smolder in his eyes had already clued her in to how he'd viewed her.

After he came in, he'd asked if he could turn her bedroom into a temporary darkroom so he could develop the pictures. She hadn't minded. And while she'd busied herself in the kitchen with baking projects and preparing the evening meal, he'd locked himself away with trays of water and chemicals.

By the time supper was ready, they'd formed a makeshift table near the sofa and Mrs. Keller to include her in the meal and conversation. Philip had been as gracious and talkative as usual except that he hadn't been quite as teasing or lighthearted.

And now, with tiredness shrouding him, she guessed he'd simply reached his limit. The hour was well past midnight. And he'd taken the burden of keeping them from freezing upon his shoulders.

"You should get some sleep." She draped his coat over the worktable so that hopefully it would dry.

"I will in a little bit." He was already gathering up an armful of the wooden stall beams that he'd chopped into pieces small enough to fit into the stove.

She approached him and began to take the load from him. "I can do this."

He halted, his tired eyes drifting across her face. "I won't be able to rest until I know that you and the Kellers are safe from the cold."

She paused in dragging a log from his hold. A deep sense of gratitude welled up within her. This man was so kind, so giving, so self-sacrificing. Her first impressions about him being a spoiled and wealthy womanizer had been wrong. So very wrong.

For whatever reason, he gave the aura that was who he was. But underneath the bluster, he was really and truly one of the nicest men she'd ever met.

"You might have everyone else fooled." She jabbed a finger against his chest, his flannel shirt cold. "But I know who you really are."

"You do?" His eyes widened and panic flitted across his face.

"Yes." She hadn't been expecting such a reaction from him, as if he was hiding something about himself.

"Then who am I?" His tone was almost demanding.

She'd meant for the interaction to be playful. But the moment wasn't exactly going the way she'd planned. She hesitated. Now that she'd started, she needed to finish. After all he'd done, the least she could do was express her thankfulness. "You hide yourself well behind your teasing and wit, but I've seen the real you—the man who walks miles in a storm, who stays up every night, who chops wood, and who won't stop, even when he's exhausted."

His expression softened. "I've been learning from you."

"No, you're already a good man and didn't need any help in learning that from me."

His lips tugged up. "Are you finally paying me a compliment?"

"Maybe."

"That wasn't so hard, was it? Not with how much there is to say about me."

And the teasing was back. She smiled just a little. "Actually, I had to scrape hard at the bottom of the barrel to find the compliment, so cherish it, because there won't be any more."

She finished helping him pick up the rest of the wood pieces, and they carried them into the front sitting room. Moments later, the fire in the stove blazed out heat. And as she took her place on the pallet near the stove, Philip laid his blankets out on the floor across from her—after unsuccessfully trying to convince Mrs. Keller to let him sit with her husband for a while.

As Philip settled in with his broad back facing her, Felicity let her eyes close in satisfaction. Now that Philip was nearby, her racing heart calmed, and she let herself drift into a peaceful sleep.

She awoke shivering, with limbs stiff from the cold.

The room was frigid, and at the clanking of the stove, she rolled to find Philip kneeling in front of the open stove door, adding fuel to low flames.

Mrs. Keller remained in her chair beside the sofa, and Mr. Keller was still sleeping underneath the heavy stack of blankets.

As the fire caught on the dry barn wood, Philip leaned

back and watched the glowing flickers. After a few moments, he closed the door and pivoted, his gaze sweeping across her.

"How is—our—supply?" She could barely get the words past her chattering teeth.

"It's adequate for now." He frowned and dropped his attention to the blanket she'd wound around her body. "I just overslept and neglected to add more fuel."

"I can—add it—next time."

His jaw flexed. "Your blanket doesn't look like it could keep a flea warm."

"Are you comparing—me to—a flea? How sweet—of you." Before she could shift the blanket closer, she lost her grip on it, since her fingers were shaking so badly.

He released a low growl. Then before she knew what he was doing, he reached for her and dragged her toward him, his arms snaking around her.

"What are—you doing?"

He held her tight and leaned back against the wall, bunching up his pallet behind him and situating her in front of him between his outstretched legs. "I'm warming you up."

"I don't need—"

"Yes, you do."

She knew she ought to protest sitting against him so closely. But he was taking charge of the situation much the same way he had the day that she'd fainted from exhaustion. How could she resist? The truth was, she was too cold to care.

He gathered up her blanket and began tucking it around her legs and arms, pinning her tightly before drawing her close against him. His arms and chest and legs folded around her like a thick down cover. And blessed warmth enveloped her.

"There. How is that?" His voice rumbled near her ear.

"Better."

"Come on. Admit it. You feel as though you're in paradise."

She did. But she wasn't about to disclose that to him. "It feels more like a sunny beach on a lake in the summer."

"Oh, so I'm a beach on a lake?"

"Or maybe a warm log on the side of a pond."

His arms tightened, then one of his hands rubbed up and down her arm.

All coherent thought fled from her mind, as it did every time his fingers grazed her. His touch was firm and the friction meant to warm her. She knew that was his intention. But suddenly all she could think about was the fact that she was sitting squarely in front of Philip, her back against his chest, his face only inches from hers. And he was touching her . . .

She leaned her head against his shoulder and relaxed into him, her legs curled up, her feet tucked under one of his legs.

She loved his touch. She couldn't deny it. The memories of his other touches lingered at the forefront of her mind, never far away. She'd pulled them out and reviewed them many times, always secretly wishing for him to caress her again.

And now, here he was, holding her. And caressing her arms.

For at least a minute, he didn't say anything. He simply rubbed her arms gently.

She wanted to snuggle into him more fully, but she didn't dare. Instead, she contented herself with breathing in the scent of him that lingered in his shirt—something that was between pine and woodsmoke.

She was embarrassed that Mrs. Keller, only a dozen paces away in the wingback chair, was witnessing Philip holding her in front of him. What must she think of the situation? That they were being indecent? Too forward? Surely Mrs. Keller would understand that, under the circumstances, the storm had driven them together.

Philip's hand slid up and down, the friction not only bringing warmth but showering her with a cascade of emotions and sensations that she wanted to bask in for the rest of the night. Maybe she would. . . . She could stay right where she was for a while. There was nothing wrong with that, was there?

He bent toward her ear. "Are you in paradise yet?"

At the hint of teasing—as if he realized how much she

enjoyed his touch—she swatted his arm and tried to wiggle away.

He chuckled and tightened his hold. "Don't go anywhere."

She pushed against him again. "This isn't decent, Philip."

"We have a chaperone, Felicity."

"I'm warm enough now, *Philip*."

"You're still shivering, *Felicity*."

She was, but only a little. Even so, as his hand glided back up her arm, she closed her eyes and sighed with the pleasure that was tingling through her arm and into her torso all the way down to her toes. She was almost purring like a kitten.

How could any one man have this much power at his fingertips? If his touch could bring her so much pleasure, what would his lips be like?

As soon as the thought came, heat raced into her face. Oh, dear heavens. What was wrong with her that she was imagining kissing Philip Berg?

After a few more moments, he brought both arms back around more fully. As his scruffy jaw scraped her skin, her lashes fell, and she drew in a shuddering breath, feeling extra sensitive to his touch.

"Try to get some sleep," he whispered.

She could only nod mutely. How would she ever be able to sleep in his arms with him so close? It would be impossible.

But as the warmth of the flames now crackling within the stove settled in around them, her eyes grew heavy, and she drifted off.

13

Philip stirred on the floor, drawing Felicity in closer.

She didn't resist. In fact, she almost seemed loath to move from the cocoon of warmth she'd found with him.

Mrs. Keller had added fuel to the stove again at some point during the night. When her rustling had awoken him and he'd started to rise, she'd motioned for him to stay where he was. "Hold her for as long as you can," she'd whispered with a nostalgic smile.

He hadn't wanted Mrs. Keller to have to get out from her blankets to refuel the stove, but he also hadn't wanted to put Felicity aside, hadn't wanted to break the connection he had with her.

Now, though the darkness was still heavy and broken only by the lantern glowing on the sofa table, he guessed that dawn wasn't too far away.

They'd survived the night. And from what he could tell, the wood was almost gone again.

He would need to go back to the barn and chop up more of the structure to see them through the day.

Should he go now?

Mrs. Keller's head bobbed in her effort to stay awake and keep the vigil with her husband.

Felicity would want him to wake her so that she could relieve the faithful woman from her duty.

Yes, it was time. Yet he loved the feel of Felicity in his arms and against his body. Her head resting against his shoulder, her hair tickling his cheek, her even breathing reminding him that he had everything he wanted or needed right here with her. If he died today, he'd die a happy man.

Actually, at this moment, on the floor of an old house in the lonesome and rugged high country of Colorado, he was happier than he ever had been in Lapland. Which begged the question—why not stay with her? Why bother going back at all? He could write to Gustaf and tell him that he intended to live in America and would never come back. Certainly if he did so, Gustaf would leave him alone, wouldn't he?

He could consider the possibility, couldn't he?

But what about the duty to his country? And to his people? If they were suffering with Gustaf as king, then how could he abandon them when it was within his power to change the course of their lives for the better?

He released a tense breath. For now, all he could do

was relish each moment with Felicity and not think beyond today. But that relishing didn't mean he could give in to the desires building inside him. And it most certainly didn't mean he could erase the boundaries he was trying to keep with her.

She released a soft breath—almost a hum of contentment. And she rustled under her blanket and pushed back against him, as if trying to find a way to burrow deeper into him.

One more tiny moment with her. That's all he'd take.

He pressed his nose into her hair and drew in a sweet honey scent. She was so soft and warm and delicate. Before he could stop himself, he pressed a kiss into the back of her head, into her loose, silky hair. As if the kiss were a key, it seemed to unlock a door he'd kept tightly closed up until this point—one that was holding back the full force of his longing. And now, desire poured out—pure, raw desire unlike anything he'd known before.

He couldn't pull away from her, so instead, he kissed her head again, this time harder. His arms wrapped around her more securely, and he had the sudden need to shift her around and find her lips so that he could kiss her thoroughly. What he wouldn't give to taste all her sweetness, to explore her, to discover if she was feeling the same longing that he was.

She stirred.

Was she sensing the change in him?

He'd done so well the past hours in keeping everything bolted away. And now the kisses to her head had undone him.

He closed his eyes and clamped his jaw, battling against his needs. He couldn't have her. Not when he had nothing to offer. If he kept going, let his desires take control, he'd turn into a selfish womanizer—the kind of man she'd hinted that he was. He couldn't—wouldn't—do that.

Holding himself immobile, he loosened his hold and sat back, trying to put some distance between them. But as he attempted to extricate himself, she turned just slightly, released a sleepy sound, and somehow her lips brushed against his neck in a sensitive spot right below his jaw.

He stilled.

From the way she remained relaxed against him, he could tell that she was mostly asleep, that she hadn't meant to brush his neck.

Even so, his skin was on fire, and the flames were spreading rapidly through his body.

"What time is it?" Her whisper grazed his skin.

This woman was going to be the end of him. "It's nearing dawn." He started to lower his mouth back to her head. Just one more kiss of her hair. That's all he'd take.

Before he could press in, she began to scramble away from him. "Dawn? Poor Mrs. Keller. She needs a respite."

Somehow his self-control was gone. It had dissipated, completely evaporated, like mist under a hot sun. His hands had a mind of their own and couldn't let go of her.

But as she pushed against him harder, the movement seemed to jar him out of his desire-laden haze. He let his arms fall away, freeing her to crawl from him and then push up until she was standing.

Underneath her coat, she was wearing the simple skirt and blouse from the previous day. And her hair was still in a lovely chignon, albeit wobbly with loose strands. For a moment, she held a hand against her forehead, as though trying to gain her bearing.

She started toward Mrs. Keller but then stopped and glanced back at him. "I don't know how we would have survived the night without you. Thank you, Philip. You've been a godsend."

He nodded mutely, unable to come up with a witty response, not with his desire blazing so hot and out of control. Yesterday, while taking pictures of her, he'd grown overheated and had to step out onto the porch for a few moments to cool himself down. But the heat then couldn't begin to compare to what he was feeling now.

He most definitely needed to go outside and douse himself with snow. Without allowing himself to take her in again, he stood, his stiff body protesting, and he made his way into the kitchen to his cold, damp outer garments. He donned them and headed outside.

The first thing he noticed as he stepped into the early light of morning was the silence. The incessant blowing had stopped, and the world around him was shrouded in a blanket of quiet white.

The second thing he realized was that the air wasn't as frigid. Yes, the temperature was still freezing, but the bitterness was gone.

As he made his way to the barn, he didn't need to hold on to the rope, and he didn't have to fight against the drifting snow. Instead, his steps made a soft swooshing that was almost pleasant. As with the other times, he had to shovel the snow away from the barn door to get inside. But without the storm, he had the way cleared in no time.

He tended to the livestock, chopped another area of the barn for fuel, and by the time he trudged back to the house, dawn had turned into daylight, with hints of sunshine peeking from behind the clouds.

Although a part of him was relieved that the worst weather had passed, another part of him wasn't ready for the time with Felicity to come to an end. Not yet. Not so soon.

From the size of the drifts, he guessed they wouldn't be safe attempting to travel until the snow melted a little. That meant he still had more time to enjoy being with her without worry of danger or without the pressure of having to leave.

As he neared the kitchen door, he paused and took in the view. With the mountains and foothills covered in snow, his breath caught at the beauty of the whitewashed world and the evergreens glistening with the ice. From the fence post draped with snow to the drifted wagon path, everything contained a pristine clarity that he wanted to capture with his camera.

Maybe today, after all the chores were done, he'd gather his camera and traipse around and get some photographs of the aftermath of the storm. But only if he could convince Felicity to join him in exploring the winter wonderland. There was no sense in denying the burning need to spend every moment possible with her while he still could.

He and Felicity alternated taking care of Mr. Keller while Mrs. Keller slept. And when he wasn't tending to the older man, he was hauling water and scrounging for dry wood. Thankfully, with the snow having stopped, he was able to locate windfall not too far from the house that was still dry enough to burn.

With the kitchen stove fueled again, Felicity made soup and biscuits. Philip ate it with a cup of coffee, never more grateful for the warm meal to settle inside and chase away the last vestiges of chill from his bones.

Finally by mid-afternoon, when Mrs. Keller had awoken and refreshed herself, Philip convinced Felicity to join him outside. The sun stayed mostly behind the clouds, but the warmth of it lingered in the air regardless.

They strapped on snowshoes, and Philip led the way to several spots that he'd wanted to photograph. With each stop, Felicity helped him set up his camera and then held the containers and lens cover while he made a lasting image of the landscape—images he would hold dearer than any of the other places he'd photographed during his travels.

During their time together, it was almost as if they'd silently agreed not to talk about the future or his leaving. Instead, she asked him astute questions about the process of taking pictures as well as the development of them. And he regaled her with tales of some of his worst moments as a photographer and his most embarrassing mistakes.

Upon her inquiry, he told her that he'd taken up the hobby of an amateur photographer during his years in boarding school because he'd been restless. He wanted to divulge that he hadn't been allowed to participate in as many of the activities as the normal students and had needed to pass the time. But he held back.

After spending so much time with her already and not having revealed his identity, he wasn't sure what purpose her knowing now would serve. It wasn't as if he was lying to her. He'd merely omitted information.

As they hiked, she wanted to hear more about his travels, both those within the United States as well as in other parts of the world. After each new place that he described, she sighed dramatically, a dreamy, faraway look filling her eyes.

He led the way back to the house through the field to the north. The curl of smoke above the evergreens ahead wafted into the evening sky, the clouds now edged with pink and lavender.

He wanted to linger and admire the beauty until darkness fell. But they needed to return and check on the Kellers as well as tend to the evening chores. And even though the temperature had been moderate enough to begin melting the snow, he was afraid he'd kept her out too long.

He lifted one snowshoe and then the next, the footwear keeping them from sinking into the deep drifts. "You should travel." He cast her a glance over his shoulder.

Her cheeks were rosy from the cold, her brown eyes were bright, and her hair was radiant against the white backdrop of snow. She looked like a snow fairy princess. Except that she leveled a stern glance at him. "Thank you for that excellent piece of advice. It was so wise and helpful."

He grinned. "I am known for doling out wisdom once in a while."

"You should do it more often. The world has been missing out."

A deep sense of contentment welled within him. He loved being with her, quite possibly more than he loved being with anyone else.

He continued for several steps before pressing forward with the conversation. "Why can't you travel? What's stopping you?"

"First, I'm a single woman—"

"That's an excuse. I've heard of an Englishwoman by the name of Isabella Bird who toured the West and the Rocky Mountains a few years ago by herself—without a chaperone or even a traveling companion."

"Really?" Felicity's question held disbelief.

"Really. Although, I'm not suggesting you do the same." Actually, at the thought of Felicity riding on a horse throughout the desolate wilderness alone, a sharp panic clutched at his gut. "In fact, I do think you should have a traveling companion."

"So should my traveling companion be another woman, or should I have a man to protect me?" Her tone held sarcasm.

His mind spun with the implications of both, and neither appealed to him, especially the prospect of her spending hours alone with another man. "Neither. At least, not with a man who isn't also your husband."

"Are you saying I'm not capable without a man?"

"No, I'm saying you're too beautiful and would draw too much unwanted attention."

"Who are you to say the attention is unwanted?"

He halted. With his knapsack and tripod slung over his shoulder, he pivoted carefully.

She stopped, too, her eyes narrowed upon him.

"Do you want other men to pay attention to you?" His voice came out gruffer than he'd intended. Was he jealous of future, unnamed men who might like her? If so, he had no right to be.

"Maybe among those men paying me attention, I'll find a husband and travel with him." She lifted her chin as though daring him to defy her.

His sights dropped to her perfect lips. A shaft of desire ripped through him. He wanted to close the distance between them and lavish kisses over her mouth. He'd show her that no other man could compare to him.

As if sensing the direction of his thoughts—or more likely seeing his desire and realizing that he wanted to kiss her—her gaze shifted to his mouth. She studied his lips like she did one of her baked creations after pulling it from the oven—hungrily.

If he could, he would let her sate herself with him. He'd let her taste him over and over. And then once she'd had her fill, he'd take his in return. Her lips would be better than any dessert, and he'd savor every tiny corner and curve.

He could only imagine what it would be like to travel with Felicity. With her, he'd never have a dull moment. Instead, when he wasn't busy kissing her senseless, they'd have fun together, laughing and teasing and helping each other to find the brighter side of life. Yet they'd also have long and meaningful conversations about important topics. And they'd argue, like they were right now, but the air would sizzle between them until he dragged her into his arms and kissed her into silence.

Why did so many of his fantasies about her involve kissing?

He swallowed the need to kiss her and was thankful the snowshoes made getting too near her awkward. "I admit, I'm already jealous of the man who will be your husband." He tried to keep his tone light.

"You should be." She didn't remove her gaze from his lips. "He's going to be a good kisser—I mean traveler." She lifted her mittened hands over her rapidly flushing cheeks, her eyes widening with mortification.

His grin kicked up. "So, you're thinking about kissing me."

"I was thinking about kissing my husband." She started forward on her snowshoes, slipping past him. "Is there anything wrong with that? Or is that forbidden to me too?"

He wanted to tell her that she was forbidden from kissing any other man but him, but his bantering about kissing was already leading him back into dangerous territory, like walking out on thin ice that was already cracking. One wrong move and he would break through and take her with him.

She was several feet in front of him, taking the lead in the hike back to the house. She moved with such confidence and strength and purpose. What man would ever be worthy of marrying her? He couldn't think of anyone. Except maybe Weston. But even he wasn't good enough. "If you're not thinking of kissing me, then you must be envisioning Weston."

She released a scoffing sound.

The noise settled his nerves. "How many times has that man proposed? Surely by now you've thought of kissing him."

"Just because a man is interested in me doesn't mean I start thinking of ways I can get him alone and pounce on him."

"Pounce?"

"You know what I mean."

"No. Enlighten me. What would *pouncing* entail?"

"Stop."

"I'm serious. Maybe you should demonstrate. I'll allow you to do so with me. I'm your willing subject."

This time she laughed lightly.

His grin worked its way free again. They walked quietly until he couldn't hold back the question burning inside him. "Why haven't you accepted his proposal yet?" The inquiry came out too seriously.

She continued on almost as if she hadn't heard him.

"Weston is a good man." He said the words that needed saying, even though he didn't want to.

"He's a very fine man."

"*Very?*"

"Any woman who marries him will be *very* blessed."

"And do you plan to be that woman?"

She walked several more feet before answering. "I don't know."

He wasn't sure why he was pressing the matter, except that he wanted her to have a happy future. Would that be with Weston?

Holding back a sigh, he followed after her, letting the matter drop and stifling the wish that she could have a happy future with him instead.

14

A snowball hit the kitchen window near the sink. It startled Felicity for only a moment before it sent a shimmy of delight through her.

She moved away from the stove and the bread she'd just taken from the oven and peered out the window into the brightness of the sunshine pouring over the melting snow.

Philip stood in the middle of the backyard, his hat and gloves on but his coat discarded. He was grinning and tossed another snowball, this one hitting the window again, the snow splattering.

She shook her head at him and pretended irritation before returning to the stove. Only then did she let her smile free as she loosened the loaf from the bread pan and placed it on the worktable to cool. A supper of stew was already simmering in the back pot, and now that the bread was done, she was free for a short while to spend time with Philip.

He called it *playing*. Already he'd thrown several other snowballs at the window, trying to get her outside to *play*. But she'd chastised him that she had too much to do and couldn't stop, even though everything within her had longed to cast aside her duties and frolic with him as she had the past two days.

After their first afternoon of taking pictures, the next day they'd trekked to the foothills on the other side of the river, and they'd sledded on a makeshift sled that he'd made out of items he'd located in the barn. She'd never been sledding before, and of course, Philip had made the experience entirely fun and enjoyable, as he did most things.

Today, on the first day of November, the temperature was warmer, especially with the sun finally coming out and deciding to stay. Although she was glad for the warmth, she dreaded losing the drifts that had prevented traveling.

She could admit she'd loved the past few days of isolated existence where she and Philip could spend endless hours together without any thought of tomorrow. But sooner or later, they would have to face what they would do when the snow melted.

Because it would melt. It already was melting. Significantly.

They might only have the rest of the day, maybe one

more, before the roads around the area became passable again.

Another snowball hit the window, followed by another.

More delight rushed through her. She untied her apron and set it on the counter before calling into the other room "Mrs. Keller? I'll be outside for a little while."

"You go on, dear." Mrs. Keller was sitting in the wingback chair beside Mr. Keller on the sofa. They hadn't returned upstairs, mostly because the fuel remained in short supply. But Felicity had also noticed the way the couple thrived in being around others, and she didn't want to relegate them to the isolation again.

The sofa wasn't as comfortable and spacious as the bed, but as long as there were no other boarders, she was all too willing to let the couple remain in the front room. She'd considered giving up her room so they could have some privacy. But she couldn't sleep upstairs near Philip. Such an arrangement wouldn't be proper.

"Enjoy that man of yours," Mrs. Keller called.

Felicity needed to correct the older woman. Philip wasn't hers. But she couldn't make herself say the words.

After all, the day was coming—likely soon—when Mrs. Keller would learn Philip wasn't hers. The thought of his leaving filled Felicity with a strange emptiness that was turning into a chasm. A deep, dark chasm.

And she was trying not to think about it.

As another snowball pinged against the glass, she crossed to the door and peeked out. "You're in big trouble for causing such a ruckus."

In the process of scooping up more snow, he rose and his eyes began to dance. "Trouble? What kind of trouble am I in, and whatever will you do with me for being so naughty?"

Oh, dear heavens. She adored him more every time he bantered with her like that. In fact, his banter was addictive. She found herself seeking it out—seeking him out—at all hours of the day and night.

She opened the door wider and stepped outside. "You'll need to come over here if you want your discipline."

He bounded through the snow toward her.

Invisible strings seemed to exist between them, irresistibly pulling them together. And as much as she wanted to touch him, needed to touch him, she tried to ignore the low, deep need. Instead, she let him approach until he stopped a foot away. Then she bent, swiped up a handful of snow, and mashed it against his face.

He stood in shocked silence, globs of snow dripping down his cheeks and chin.

Her laughter bubbled out.

He watched her for a moment. Then he lunged for her.

She was expecting it and dodged out of his grasp. She

pivoted, then, holding up her skirt, she darted across the yard and away from him.

He started after her, but in the next instant he slipped and fell to his knees.

She laughed even more, tramping in the snow as fast as her feet would carry her.

"That wasn't very nice discipline," he called after her as he pushed himself back to his feet.

"It's what you deserved."

"Maybe. But now you're the one in trouble." His eyes were alight with challenge, like a skilled hunter closing in on his prey, daring her to escape but warning her that he wouldn't let her get away.

A thrill curled inside her all the way down to her toes. "I'm so frightened of you."

"You should be scared, especially with what I have planned." He started after her, but his heavier boots in the wet snow seemed to slow him down so that she had time to race farther ahead.

"You're too slow and won't be able to catch me." She taunted him as she grabbed a handful of snow. Taking aim, she tossed it at him.

It smacked against his chest—not hard, but enough to send slush dripping down his flannel shirt.

He scooped up snow and, in one easy motion, made a snowball and threw it at her. The hit was gentle, but the splotch clung to her blouse. He was already throwing another before she had the wherewithal to fight him back.

"I guess this means war." She ducked away from his missile and launched one back.

"Oh yes." He knelt and began shaping another snowball. "When I win, what reward will you give me?"

"You won't win." She veered toward a fence post by the garden and ducked behind.

"I'll win, and I'll expect a prize when I do."

"And if you lose—which you will—then you will owe me a prize." She busily began making snowballs of her own, her body charged with the energy and life she always felt when she was with him. How could being with him—playing with him—feel so freeing?

Was it that she took life so seriously most of the time? She'd been striving so hard to keep up with the workload, to be productive, and to remain put together. Something deep inside had always driven her to be better. Maybe it was the echo of her mother's voice reminding her that she needed to strive harder. Or maybe it was her own inadequacy from past failures that pushed her to try to be good enough.

Whatever the case, she hadn't often stopped to simply enjoy life with all its imperfections. Somehow, with Philip, she was doing that. He was showing her how to embrace the present. And he seemed to be accepting her for who she was, in spite of all her shortcomings.

At first, the snowball fight went her way. She was able

to fire off two rounds for every one of his. And since he was out in the open, she hit him nearly every time—until he finally stood to his full height and began to approach her, letting each hit bounce off him as if she were throwing light wisps of cotton at him instead of slushy snow.

With each step he drew closer, he kept tossing snow at her, but his aim always landed in front of her. When he towered over her, she stood and planted her hands on her hips. "You went easy on me and let me win, didn't you?"

He held up his hands as though to prove his innocence. And his blue eyes, more beautiful than the cloudless sky overhead, were filled with sunshine. "Why would I do a thing like that?"

"Because you're treating me like a fine, breakable teacup."

"Or maybe it's because I want to be the one to owe you a prize." His tone dipped in his seductive, smooth-talking way.

It made her stomach dip too. "If I'm the winner, I get to pick the prize."

"No. I get to give it."

"That's not fair. What if I don't like my reward?"

"Oh, you'll like it." He did it again. Lowered his voice and made her feel as though she were walking a high mountain trail with thinning air that made her lightheaded.

She pushed against his chest, needing to somehow diffuse the tension pulling more magnetically with each passing moment.

At her light shove, he pretended to tumble backward. At the same time, he latched onto her arm and pulled her with him. With a grin, he allowed himself to fall down into the snow. And he didn't release her, so that she found herself landing backward in a soft drift close by.

"This is your prize." He began to move his arms and legs, shifting them in and then out. "Making snow angels."

Her backside was soaking in the wet snow, but she pushed herself up to her elbows and watched him. After a moment, he gingerly crawled away from his spot on the ground, leaving behind an imprint—one that did, indeed, look like that of an angel.

"Your turn." He waited expectantly above her.

She hesitated only a moment before she lowered herself back to the snow and began to shift her arms and legs the way he'd done. When finished, she inched away and then stood and examined her snow angel. Hers was directly beside his, giving the impression that the two were holding hands—or wings.

"Our guardian angels are watching over us." He was staring down at their indentations in the snow, his expression almost tender.

It truly was beautiful to see his larger imprint and her

smaller one beside it, both looking like angels.

"Let's do it again." She tugged him toward an untouched patch of snow only a few feet away. Before she could position herself, he reached for her hand and slipped his fingers around hers.

Her body halted its forward momentum, and she felt as though she stood in front of a narrow tunnel where he was the only thing she could see and his hand was the only thing she could focus on.

He hadn't held her hand before. Yes, he'd tugged at her arm or guided her by her shoulders or poked at her playfully. But he hadn't purposefully held on to her for any length of time.

Of course, he'd deliberately grazed her on a couple occasions. And those occasions had seared into her, rendering her a quivering bundle of nerves. Even though she couldn't deny how much she liked his touch, she was also relieved he'd been a gentleman and hadn't taken advantage of her or their being snowed in together.

But now, holding her hand? What did it mean? She opened her mouth to question him, but no words came out.

He held himself precariously, starting to tip backward into the drift. "Ready?"

"No—" She was too late. He was falling and taking her with him.

His fingers were surprisingly warm, even though he'd

been throwing snow at her. And they were strong with a hint of gentleness.

With her thoughts focused on the feel of his hand holding hers, she didn't pay attention to where she was landing. And a moment later, she fell backward directly into him, almost squarely on top of him.

"Oomph." He flinched at the impact.

For a second, she couldn't fathom anything else and lay unmoving on top of him. Her whole focus was on the feel of his hand against hers, their palms touching, his long fingers draped around hers possessively, his grip tightening.

He didn't move or say anything either. Finally, he cleared his throat. "Umm, I guess you missed the snow."

Something in his tone penetrated her mind. And suddenly she was keenly aware of his solid body beneath hers—his broad chest, his sinewy arms, and his long legs tangled with hers.

Ugh. Mortification swept through her at the indecency of her position. She was directly on top of him, likely cutting off his breathing.

She tried to roll off, but because of the way he was holding her hand so tightly, she found herself flipped over, and this time her chest—instead of her back—pressed into him.

More mortification swept through her. She was still on top of him but this time staring down at him, his face inches from hers, his wide eyes peering up at her.

"Oh, dear heavens." She tried to make herself move but didn't make it far. "I'm sorry, Philip. I didn't mean for this to happen—"

He cut her off with a finger to her lips from his free hand.

The caress sent a needy surge through her middle. And suddenly her senses were overwhelmed with not only his hand in hers but also his finger against her mouth. He held it there for a moment before moving it away.

"You should have warned me you wanted to tackle me instead of make snow angels." His tone came out teasing.

"I didn't mean to tackle you." Where was her wit? And why couldn't she breathe?

"I think you did." His lips turned up slyly.

"I wasn't paying attention. That's all."

"Likely excuse—"

"It's not an excuse."

"Just admit it. You tackled me because you want to kiss me."

He'd teased her about kissing before. And while those conversations had warmed up her insides, she had always been able to tease him back.

This time, she couldn't find a retort. Instead, her attention dropped to his mouth. It was only inches away, his lips still curved. Firm and full. What would it be like to touch his lips the way he'd touched hers?

No, she didn't want to kiss him. She wouldn't even think about it. But she could touch him, couldn't she? And find out exactly how those lips of his felt beneath her fingertips.

She lifted her free hand to his face, and then before she could talk herself out of it, she brought her fingers down lightly against his lips.

His smile disappeared.

Had she made a mistake?

She tore her attention from his mouth only to find her gaze colliding with his. The mirth was gone, and the blue was quickly darkening and his pupils widening. She wasn't an expert on reading emotions, but she had no trouble deciphering stark desire in those dark depths.

What had she done? He'd been keeping the moment light and full of teasing as he always did. She should have joked back, should have smiled, should have rolled off like she'd been trying to do.

Instead, she'd parked on top of him as if he were a mountaintop and she intended to stay for a while and have a picnic. She couldn't. She had to disentangle her fingers from his. That was the first place she had to start. Then her mind would be clearer, and she'd be able to make better decisions.

She tugged at her hand, loosening it from his hold. But before she could extricate it all the way, he lifted it to his lips, brushing a soft kiss against her knuckles.

All of time stopped from the beginning of the world to the end.

His eyes caught hers again, refusing to let go. And this time, as he laid another soft kiss on her hand, her pulse halted, and all that mattered was this man. Philip Berg was everything she'd ever wanted—kindhearted, giving, self-sacrificing, caring, decent, good, and a dozen other qualities that she couldn't find words for at the moment.

And he was also everything she'd never known she wanted—funny, teasing, talkative, interesting, adventurous, lighthearted . . . and yes, even playful.

The truth was, she liked him more than she ever had any other man she'd met. Dare she say she might even be falling in love with him? She knew without a doubt that if he asked her to leave with him, she would want to go. She'd even marry him.

The realization hit her with a frightening force. She'd said no to every other suitor who'd proposed to her for the past year and a half. And here she was, ready to marry the one man who hadn't proposed, who hadn't made any mention of a commitment to her.

He kissed her hand again, with an adoration that bordered on reverence. Then, with warm tenderness, he began to make a trail of soft kisses toward her wrist.

Each brush of his lips filled her with a swirl of sensations that made her feel as if she was falling.

Yes, she was falling in love with him. Not only did she like who he was as a person, but she also was attracted to him physically. The pull she felt toward him—especially in moments like this, where he was holding her so intimately—was overpowering. The soft brush of his mouth and caress of his breath took her captive, made her his willing prisoner, and took away every thought but needing him.

She needed him.

As if hearing her thoughts, he paused above her wrist. Something in his eyes—the seriousness, the intensity—wrapped around her and bound her even more. Did he need her the same way?

If so, what was holding him back? Even though she liked the playful side of him, there had been too many times when they'd been starting to get serious that he'd changed the mood with a lighthearted comment, teasing, or even a funny action. She'd begun to suspect it was his way of deflecting and not letting himself grow too attached to her.

But why? What was wrong with her that he didn't want to get closer? Wasn't she good enough for a man like him?

And what about now? What if he pulled away again? Maybe she needed to make it very clear that she cared about him. If she bent in and brushed a kiss against his lips, then he'd have no doubts about how she felt . . .

Yet, after allowing that disastrous kiss a few years ago with her best friend's brother, she'd kept her vow not to let another suitor kiss her. Of course, in this case, if *she* began the kiss—instead of the suitor—then she technically wouldn't be breaking her vow, would she? She'd be taking charge, the one giving the kiss. Not him.

As his open mouth connected with her throbbing pulse, she nearly swooned.

Before she could talk herself out of her resolve, she tugged her hand away from his and, in the same motion, spanned the distance between them. Closing her eyes, she grazed her lips against his.

He stilled.

She wasn't knowledgeable about kissing. Her first and last kiss had been short and sloppy.

Even so, she let her lips linger against Philip's, the softness and warmth grazing her.

He didn't press in, but neither did he pull away. Was that a good sign?

His lips were slightly open, and she let hers open, too, as she nudged his mouth again with hers, wanting more from the kiss, wanting more from him. At the same time, a tremor of fear stole through her.

Yes, she'd sensed his desire, had seen it in his eyes. But that didn't mean he wanted to kiss her.

She hesitated. Ugh. What was she doing? She'd made a mistake . . .

She started to break away, but before she could, his hand looped behind her neck, holding her in place, and then he chased after her lips and totally and completely took possession of them.

He'd clearly been holding himself back for whatever reason. And now he moved urgently, pressing in, meshing his lips with hers, a hint of desperation tinging his kisses. He was like the medieval knight she'd imagined him to be, charging forward and capturing her. His plundering stirred her appetite for more of him, so that she wanted nothing more than to feel his body against hers.

It was a wanton thought, but the longing was keen. And she glided her hands over his perfectly sculpted chest, letting her fingers skim his flesh, which was all too accessible since his shirt was wet and plastered to him.

His hand at her neck threaded into her hair, which had come loose at some point during their playing. His other hand shifted to her hip, his fingers splaying and tugging her more directly on top of him, almost as if he was feeling the need to be closer to her too. In the same moment, the rhythm of his mouth turned more urgent and pulsed with need.

She couldn't breathe, and she couldn't hold back a soft moan.

"Felicity?" The call penetrated the haze of passion that surrounded her.

Beneath her, Philip stirred and clearly had heard the

voice. But his kiss was too passionate, too fervent, too consuming for her to break away. And he made no move to bring the kiss to an end either.

"Felicity? What is going on here?" This time the voice was almost directly behind her, and it roused her from the blissful dream she'd been living in. One in which she and Philip were the only people who existed in the entire world.

Even though she didn't want to awaken, and even though she didn't want to stop, there was something in the newcomer's tone that drew her back to reality. Was it shock?

She'd been the one to start the kiss, and now she had to utilize control and be the one to finish it. She had to tear her lips from Philip's. She had to open her eyes and return to the real world. But try as she might to force herself away from him, she couldn't.

"I can't believe this." The person's shadow fell across them along with a wagonload of censure.

The voice didn't belong to Mrs. Keller. And it didn't even belong to her sister, Patience. Instead, it was deep and manly.

With a final lingering kiss, Philip tugged against her lips in a way that made her nearly lose her mind. Then he broke from her, shifted his head, and smiled up at the man. "Hello, Weston."

15

The sun blinded Philip as he peered up at Weston Oakley, standing above him and Felicity.

Philip knew he should've pulled away from Felicity and ended the kiss the first time he'd heard Weston call out her name. But something had driven him to keep on kissing her—something hot and possessive, something that wanted to prove Felicity belonged to him.

The need to do so was unreasonable. Because Felicity didn't belong to him—couldn't belong to him—and needed to belong to Weston.

So why had he continued the kiss? And why was he now making no effort to extricate himself from her?

Felicity didn't move from on top of him either. She seemed incapable, as if in a stupor. Instead, she rested with her full weight pressing in, her face still inches from his, her exhalations heavy against his mouth. With her lips swollen and her chest rising and falling against his, desire continued to pump through his blood.

He hadn't expected his kisses upon her hand to lead to this passionate moment. He'd only meant for a brief moment of tenderness between them as they'd had on a couple of other occasions.

But she'd taken him by surprise when, instead of rolling away from him, she'd bent in and touched her lips lightly to his. When she'd held her lips there, he'd known her move hadn't been accidental, that she'd purposefully initiated the kiss.

For a second or two, he hadn't known what to do, hadn't wanted to take things further. Instead, he'd intended to keep the relationship between them from getting too serious, as he always did. Yet, with her lips against his so sweetly and gently, she'd swept him into a world of such pure bliss that his body had responded with a powerful urge, one that he'd been fighting all along and could no longer resist.

The truth was, he'd been denying himself since meeting her. Though he'd used incredible willpower— had tried to hold himself back, tried to convince himself he didn't care, tried to keep the barriers he'd erected— he'd no longer been able to ignore the sharp yearning to have this beautiful woman for himself.

Need had welled up within him so forcefully that he'd lost his sense of reason. All his work to keep a tight rein on his emotions and protect Felicity from himself flew from his mind. He'd hesitated only a moment before greedily taking her offering, not wanting her to get away, not ready for her to release him before he had the chance to thoroughly explore her with a kiss.

He'd rationalized that one kiss wouldn't harm either of them. One small kiss . . .

But he should have known it wouldn't be one small kiss. Not after the past weeks of stuffing all his feelings for her into a compartment at the back of his mind. Instead, his feelings had come rushing out, crashing over him and enveloping him.

The cold snow against his back had soaked his clothing and should have chilled his flesh. And yet his body was hot, and his breath was still heavy in his chest with need still coursing through his blood.

Weston had taken off his hat and jabbed his hand into his dark hair. He was glowering down at Philip as if he intended to yank him to his feet and begin using him as a bullseye for target practice.

Wait. Weston was *here*.

Philip shifted his head to Weston's horse a dozen paces away.

That meant the snow had melted enough that a horse could get around. Maybe not easily, but transportation was possible.

In fact, all throughout the day and even during their snowball fight and snow-angel making, a nagging in his conscience had told him that he was delaying unnecessarily, that he could probably go today. At the very least he had to make an effort to ride into town.

The truth was, the few days of being marooned at the boardinghouse were over.

Philip kept his grin in place and crossed his arms behind his head. "Nice of you to stop by and finally check on Felicity as I requested of you."

Weston's scowl deepened. "What are you doing here in Fairplay? Ain't you supposed to be long gone?"

"It's a good thing I didn't leave. Someone had to be available to help Felicity survive the storm, especially since you didn't come check on her." His accusation was a low blow. The storm had been too dangerous for anyone to venture out. Even so, Philip couldn't stop himself from riling up the man.

"Whoa now. I set out to her place several times." Weston's gaze shifted to Felicity, who still hadn't budged from where she was sprawled over him. "But couldn't make it more than a dozen steps before having to turn back."

As though finally hearing Weston's voice, Felicity glanced over her shoulder. Her eyes rounded at the sight of him, and she began to scramble off Philip. She pushed up, her face flushing and mortification filling her eyes. Whatever trance he'd held over her with his touch and his kissing, she was waking up from it and realizing the indecency of their situation.

He needed to move, needed to stand up, needed to help her. More than that, he had to admit to Weston that the kissing had been a fluke. That it hadn't meant anything and that it wouldn't happen again.

That was the truth. The kissing had been innocent, and there was nothing else going on. But even though the words pressed for release, Philip swallowed them, that strange need swelling up to prove Felicity was his and no other man's. It was an irrational thought, but he couldn't shake it.

Weston, ever chivalrous, reached out and carefully assisted Felicity to her feet, eyes radiating hurt and betrayal. "Has Philip been staying here this whole time?"

Felicity hesitated then nodded. "He arrived just as the storm was starting, covered in ice and half frozen. I couldn't send him away."

"Couldn't? Or wouldn't?"

"It was too dangerous. Too icy. We didn't expect one night to turn into five."

"You shoulda left." Weston quickly shifted the blame and glared again at Philip, which was fine with him. He'd rather have Weston angry at him than at Felicity.

"I took you for a gentleman of honor," Weston continued. "Reckon I was wrong, and you're nothin' more than a scoundrel and a scallywag. If you've hurt Felicity, so help me, I'll send you out of town in a casket."

"Nothing has happened between us, Weston." Felicity's cheeks remained flushed—from embarrassment or the pleasure of the kiss?

Philip mentally slapped himself. It didn't matter if she'd liked the kiss. Or at least, it shouldn't matter.

"I assure you," Felicity continued earnestly, "nothing like this has happened before today—before now. Philip has been a true gentleman the entire time that he's been here."

"I ain't a blind man." Weston's voice was unrelentingly hard. "Reckon what I saw makes things plenty clear that this fella ain't a gentleman."

Philip reclined and crossed his legs at his ankles now too. "And I also assure you that one of the top behaviors of any true gentleman is knowing how to kiss well." It wasn't, but he had to say something to defuse the tension. "And I have no doubt that if the situation had been reversed, you would have taken Felicity's offer of a kiss just as readily as I did."

Felicity's offer of a kiss. The words hung in the air.

Weston seemed to make sense of what Philip had insinuated—that Felicity had been the one to start the kiss, not him. His dark eyes shot to her and filled with hurt. Was he thinking of how long he'd pursued her but how she'd never once initiated a kiss?

Philip hoped so and was ashamed to admit it.

Felicity squirmed and stared down at her wet boots.

Weston took a step back. "I can see plain as day that my help ain't needed here. Reckon I'll hop on out of the way."

Felicity held her hand toward him. "Weston, wait. Please let me explain."

"I don't need an explanation, sweetheart. Clear as an empty whiskey bottle you don't want me. I'm just a fool for letting myself have Cupid's cramp as long as I did."

"You weren't a fool."

"Yep, reckon I let my hankering get the best of me."

"You're a good man—"

Weston slapped his hat back on his head. "If I'm so blasted good, then why weren't you able to start caring about me in all the months I've been trying to get my loop around you, but you could start caring about this fancy fella in no time at all?"

Weston's question was a good one, and Philip wanted to hear Felicity's answer. He settled back, his arms still behind his head, even though the snow was starting to penetrate past his desire and make him feel the cold.

Felicity opened her mouth to respond but then stopped.

Weston waited, his eyes fairly pleading with Felicity to answer him and make the situation go away and be alright.

But after another moment, she lowered her head. "I'm sorry, Weston."

What was she apologizing for? Was she telling Weston she was sorry that she couldn't care about him? That things wouldn't be able to work out between them?

Whatever it was, Weston didn't like it. He shook his head, then spun and walked toward his horse, whose reins were hanging loose, as if hastily dismounted.

How much of their kissing had Weston witnessed as he'd come riding down the lane? No doubt he'd spotted them lying together in the backyard as he'd neared the house and stomped right over. How could he have missed the passion and the fervor?

For the briefest of moments, Philip couldn't keep from gloating. But at the distress that was quickly filling Felicity's face as she watched Weston walk off, a sliver of guilt pricked him. He shouldn't be happy that Felicity was finally cutting things off with Weston—which was what she was doing, wasn't it? He ought to be feeling some contrition for being the cause of their parting. If only he could manufacture remorse . . .

Felicity started after Weston, her damp skirt tangling in her legs as though attempting to trip her. Philip half hoped the tangling would keep her from going. Weston wouldn't be able to resist her with her damp blouse plastered to her skin and her red hair hanging loose.

Even soggy and wet, Felicity had never looked more beautiful.

Philip wanted to stand up, race after her, pull her

back into his arms, and kiss her again until she forgot all about Weston. When finished with that, he wanted to soothe all her problems, tell her everything would be alright, and that in the end he'd be with her. But the reality of the situation pinned him to the ground. He had no right to her. And he had no right to interfere in her relationship with Weston.

Philip finally pushed himself up to a sitting position, the weight of responsibility prodding him to rectify the situation. He ought to go after Weston and assure him Felicity would still learn to care for him if he remained patient. He'd make sure Weston knew Felicity wasn't really his, that he'd made a mistake in kissing her and would never do it again. That whatever was happening between them was fleeting and coming to an end.

Weston represented permanence, safety, and stability. All the things Felicity needed. All the things Philip was not.

She trailed after the fellow, slipping and sliding in the snow. But Weston had already mounted and was jerking on the reins in his haste to get away. No doubt he was not only angry but embarrassed. Hopefully, once he'd had time to think about the situation, he'd realize he had no competition from any other man in the high country, not even Philip. And once Philip left, Felicity would realize it too.

As Weston trotted down the lane away from the

house, Felicity stood rigidly watching him. He didn't turn back around, and when he disappeared from sight, she hung her head and slowly walked toward the front of the house. A moment later, the door banged closed.

The door banged closed inside of Philip too. Weston hadn't been the fool. No, Philip had been the fool. He'd let himself feel things for Felicity he had no business feeling.

He stood, brushing off the slush that clung to his trousers. He hadn't meant to make a mess of things for Felicity. But that's what he'd done by being with her.

Of course, he didn't regret that he'd come to her farm that day of the ice storm and had been with her during the fuel shortage to help her survive. He shuddered at what might have happened if he hadn't been there.

But it was time for him to go. As hard as it would be, he had to stop dallying. He had to leave before it became impossible to do so.

16

Felicity's stomach churned. It had ever since Weston had ridden away. And it had only gotten worse when Philip had silently entered the house, ascended to his room, changed his clothing, and ridden away too.

Where had he gone? And why had he left without an explanation?

She glanced out the front window and down the lane, now almost completely melted under the warmth of the afternoon sunshine.

Her heart trembled at the thought that he was riding to town and making plans to leave. Or maybe he'd gone after Weston to try to keep him from spreading rumors about her indiscretion.

She turned away from the window and paced through the sitting room. In a chair next to the sofa, Mrs. Keller watched her with raised brows. Mr. Keller, during one of the rare times he was awake, followed her with curious eyes.

Felicity was relieved Mrs. Keller wasn't a busybody and had the decency not to bring up anything about the situation with Philip. Of course, the dear woman had likely heard Weston arrive on his horse. She'd probably watched out the window as he'd approached the front door but then veered toward the backyard. Even if Mrs. Keller didn't know about the kiss, she could surely guess that Weston hadn't been pleased to find Philip at the boardinghouse.

"I'll go check on supper." Felicity spoke the words to no one in particular as she headed into the kitchen. But even as she crossed to the stove, lifted the lid, and sniffed the soup, her mind couldn't register what kind of soup it was or any of the scents emanating from it. In fact, the past couple of hours had been such a blur that Felicity couldn't remember what she'd cut up and put in the pot, and she didn't care.

She set the lid back in place, stepped over to the worktable, and patted the loaf of bread she'd made earlier in the day, which seemed a lifetime ago.

Pressing a hand against her forehead, she blew out a taut breath. "What have I done?"

She didn't need to ask. She already knew. She'd kissed Philip Berg. And she'd allowed Weston Oakley to ride away, essentially putting an end to his courting her.

She hated hurting Weston. But now he knew they weren't meant to be together. And if she'd harbored any thoughts—even slim—about one day being with Weston, she no longer did. She'd thought she wasn't ready for a relationship with any man. But maybe she'd just needed the right man.

Even so, she never would have believed she could be so bold as to initiate a kiss. It had been unexpected and unplanned.

She released a long sigh and started pacing the length of the kitchen.

Whatever the case, what was done was done. And now she had to live with the repercussions.

What had Philip thought of their kiss? What did it mean to him?

She'd wanted to ask him, wanted to tell him she was falling in love with him, wanted to beg him not to leave. But at the same time, she didn't want to pressure him. She certainly didn't want to coerce him into staying with her here in Fairplay. He didn't have to agree to marry her or anything serious like that. But would he consider staying for the winter and seeing how their relationship developed?

After kissing her the way he had, he had to be feeling some of the same things she was. It had to be more than just physical attraction for him. Surely he liked her and wanted to be with her too.

Or was that just wishful thinking?

She paused in front of the door to her bedroom that

was off the kitchen. It was still Philip's makeshift darkroom. He'd given her a tour shortly after setting up the room, showing her the various stages of photograph development. He'd even let her try her hand at developing one of the pictures of the snowy landscape.

Now as she opened the door a sliver, she let her eyes adjust to the darkness of the room, the lone window covered by a black cloth. The chemicals and trays and plates and lines of drying paper still filled the room.

He'd shown her the pictures from the rest of his travels in the United States—photographs from Oregon, Washington, California, Nevada, and Utah. He had some from the western part of Colorado before he'd ventured into South Park.

After Denver, he didn't have plans for where they would go. Possibly St. Louis. Maybe New Orleans. Even Florida for the duration of the winter.

She couldn't deny that she envied the ease with which Philip and Declan could travel. They not only had the financial capability to do so, but they needed no chaperone, could move with ease, and had few worries. If only the logistics were simpler for a single woman. And if only she were braver, like the Englishwoman who'd traveled on her own.

Even if she were braver, she'd never leave the Kellers to fend for themselves. They—and others like them—were the reason she had to keep the boardinghouse open.

At the faint clopping of horse hooves on the path leading to the house, her heart gave an extra thud. Philip was home.

Home? She shook her head. This wasn't his home. And yet it was all too easy to pretend that it was, especially with how well he'd fit into her life during his stay. Not only had he helped share the burden of all the responsibilities, but his presence had become such a natural part of her existence that she wasn't sure how she could go back to living without him there.

She closed the door to the bedroom. Then she smoothed her hair back, tucking the stray strands into the knot before straightening the clean and dry blouse she'd changed into after he'd left for town.

Should she run out and greet him and blurt out how she felt about him and ask him to stay? A part of her wanted to throw caution aside and be spontaneous, the way Philip sometimes was. But the other part of her clung tightly to the security that came from being controlled and careful and cautious.

As the plodding of the horse drew nearer, she rushed to the stove and began to stir the soup, needing something to occupy her hands and to prove to Philip that she hadn't been obsessing over him—over them—the entire time he'd been gone, even though she had been.

The horse halted in front of the house instead of continuing on to the barn. Did he intend to go out again?

Her spoon came to a halt. Or maybe he was planning to leave the boardinghouse tonight and move back into town. With the Kellers being there, she and Philip certainly weren't alone and living in sin. But the rumors were sure to abound, just as they had for Charity and Hudson—especially if Weston said anything about seeing them kissing.

It probably would be for the best if Philip lived in Fairplay for the winter. He could court her in a proper fashion, visiting in the evenings. Or she could see him when she rode into town.

As footsteps tapped up the porch steps, she made her way into the front room. Mr. and Mrs. Keller were both waiting for her expectantly, and Mrs. Keller offered her an encouraging smile.

At a soft, almost timid knock against the door, Felicity halted midway through the room. Such tapping didn't belong to Philip. When he knocked—which wasn't often—his was harder and more demanding.

Felicity crossed the final distance, hoping she was wrong—that it was Philip after all, that he was simply knocking lightly so that he didn't disturb the Kellers. But as she swung open the door, she wasn't surprised to see someone else.

A petite woman stood on the porch holding a toddler on her hip. Pretty green eyes met Felicity's shyly amidst a delicately-boned face surrounded by light-brown hair that was braided beneath a simple bonnet.

The woman studied Felicity's face with interest. "Miss Courtney?"

"Yes, I am she."

The toddler, a little boy who didn't seem older than two, lifted his head off his mother's shoulder to peer at Felicity with curiosity too. He had the same light-brown hair, only a shade fairer, and it was as straight and wispy as straw.

The woman reached into her coat pocket and removed a folded piece of paper. As she began to open it up, Felicity recognized the information on the front. It was the advertisement for help that she'd posted around town.

"I saw the notice before the storm, but I wasn't able to ride out until today." The woman spoke softly. "I hope I'm not too late to apply for your position."

Felicity couldn't keep from giving the woman a once-over, taking in the gloves, thick cloak, and the fine gown, which was a little worn and bedraggled but still fashionable. Even though she was smaller in size, she seemed healthy and strong—if carrying her toddler was any indication.

Even so, the advertisement was specifically for a man. The notice said so in bold print: *A man who can come out to the boardinghouse once a day to tend to the livestock, chop wood, haul water, and other labor as needed.*

Felicity glanced behind the woman to find a fine horse with bulging saddlebags, as well as a carpetbag secured behind the saddle. "I haven't filled the position. But as you can see from my advertisement, I'm looking for a man."

"I can do the work of a man." She spoke the words quickly, as if she'd rehearsed them. "I'm quite good at tending to livestock, chopping wood, hauling water, and any other work that needs to be done."

Maybe the woman hadn't just rehearsed what she planned to say—maybe she'd also memorized the advertisement. A quiet desperation seemed to stiffen the woman's body as she waited for Felicity's pronouncement.

The fact was, Felicity didn't know if she would need the help anymore. If Philip stayed in the area, then he'd be more than willing to assist as needed just as he'd been doing. "I'm sorry, Mrs. . . . ?"

She glanced over her shoulder, then dropped her voice. "Mrs. Taylor. Serena Taylor." She had a Southern accent.

Felicity scanned the homestead yard and the lane leading back to town. Was someone chasing after Mrs. Taylor? Was she in some kind of danger? Or maybe she was simply struggling to support her child without a husband.

Felicity stepped outside and closed the door. "What

about your husband, Mrs. Taylor? Is he looking for work too?"

Her gaze shot to her son, who had returned his head to her shoulder before she lowered her voice to a whisper. "My husband is . . . deceased." When Mrs. Taylor stumbled over the word and then didn't meet Felicity's gaze, it was all too easy to see that the woman was hiding something.

Felicity was tempted to confront her about it. She valued truth and forthrightness for herself and expected it in others. And yet, as Mrs. Taylor gently brushed a kiss against her son's forehead, compassion stirred within Felicity for this pretty young woman and her child.

What if Mrs. Taylor was facing some sort of difficulty with her husband? Or if the man truly was gone, then perhaps she'd come upon hard times. This job might be her last option.

Felicity pressed her lips together to keep from asking more questions. If the woman was in a crisis, then she was exactly the kind of person they hoped to help at their boardinghouse.

The truth, they'd always been generous with those who were in need. They'd allowed people to live there, even when they couldn't pay their fees on time, even when it took weeks for them to be able to afford the home.

Even though Charity and Patience wouldn't approve

of having another boarder, surely they would understand that she couldn't turn this woman away, just as she hadn't been able to turn away the Kellers.

Mrs. Taylor hefted her little boy and then squared her shoulders. "I realize I'm not what you were expecting, Miss Courtney. But please give me a chance. I promise you won't be disappointed."

Again, Felicity scanned the woman's garments as well as her child's. Everything about them, even the leather bag on the back of the horse, spoke of wealth and privilege. Something had obviously happened to change Mrs. Taylor's fortune. And now she was clearly at the mercy of strangers for survival.

"Where have you been staying?"

As if sensing Felicity's hesitancy, Mrs. Taylor continued. "Tate was sick for a bit, and so I have been living at one of the hotels for the past weeks."

At the mention of his name, the boy lifted his head and peered up at his mother.

She pressed a kiss against the boy's forehead before turning her pleading eyes upon Felicity again. "I guarantee, if you hire me for a dollar a day, I'll do everything you ask of me and more."

"Mrs. Taylor, I believe you will, but—"

"Please." The woman's voice dropped with a note of panic. "Please. You won't regret it."

Felicity wanted to reach out and squeeze the woman's

hand to reassure her that she had nothing to worry about, but she couldn't make that kind of promise. "I would like to hire you to help at the boardinghouse, but would you consider other terms?"

"Yes, of course." The response fell from the woman's lips and was loaded with relief.

"Instead of a dollar a day—"

"Then seventy-five cents a day." Her demand was soft, and she stared at the ground as she spoke it. "The hotel charges me fifty cents a day for the room, and we can survive with twenty-five cents for food."

Felicity could relate to the despair of living so meagerly. She'd had to do it on more than one occasion. And the uncertainty and fears were difficult to live with, more so than the lack of provisions.

"I'm not communicating well, Mrs. Taylor." Felicity smiled. "I was hoping you'd be willing to live here at the boardinghouse in exchange for room and board as well as compensation for your work."

Mrs. Taylor drew in a shaky breath as if preparing to argue more, but then she stopped and stared at Felicity, her eyes widening and filling with tears. "I'll do it."

"Don't you want to hear the nature of your work before you agree to the terms?"

"I'll do anything, and if I don't know how to do it, I promise I'll learn. I'm a quick learner."

"I'm hoping you might be willing to consider helping

to nurse one of my boarders who is an invalid." Felicity briefly explained the situation with the Kellers, and before she could finish, Mrs. Taylor's eyes were again brimming with tears, and some spilled over. "The work sounds absolutely perfect, if you're sure my son won't be a bother."

"I actually believe your son will be a blessing to Mr. Keller. He'll enjoy having more company."

Mrs. Taylor's expression radiated relief and a measure of happiness. "You're the kindest, sweetest woman I have ever met, Miss Courtney—"

"Call me Felicity."

"Then please, call me Serena."

"You clearly haven't met my sisters if you think I'm the kindest and sweetest woman, because I can't even begin to compare with them."

Serena smiled through her tears. "I do hope I have the opportunity to meet them too."

As Felicity led Serena inside, she explained more about her sisters and their new marriages and living situations. She introduced her to the Kellers, then helped her bring in her meager possessions and situated her in the third bedroom upstairs.

Tate clung to Serena and hardly let his mother put him down for a minute before clamoring to be picked up again.

"He's just shy." Serena tenderly combed her son's hair

back from his face and kissed his cheek as they returned to the front room. "Once he has the chance to get used to everyone, he'll be fine."

"I'm sure he will." Mrs. Keller smiled at the little boy, her eyes shining with the delight of having the mother and son staying at the boardinghouse.

Before Felicity could say anything else, the pounding of more horse hooves wrenched her attention away from the new boarder toward the window and the sight of Philip riding down the lane.

He had his bowler pulled low, shadowing his face so that she couldn't read his expression. Was he happy to be back? Was he eager to see her again?

Her pulse began to tick faster, as though time itself was speeding up and urging her to go out and be with him. "Mrs. Keller, would you mind taking over with Serena and explaining Mr. Keller's care to her?" She was already moving toward the door and didn't wait for a response before exiting the house onto the porch.

Philip had already passed by and was nearing the barn, likely to tend to the gelding. Serena's horse, still tied to the hitching post in front of the house, needed to be cared for. If Felicity took the horse to the barn, she'd be able to speak with Philip without everyone else being able to listen to their conversation.

But what should she talk to him about? Did she really dare to bring up their kiss and ask him what it meant to him? He was an open person, wasn't usually afraid to discuss important topics. Surely he'd be willing to speak about their future.

She made quick work of guiding Serena's horse to the barn. The afternoon sun would soon fade into evening, and the day would be spent. Would it be one of Philip's last at the boardinghouse, or could they figure out a way to make it one of his first?

As she neared the open entrance of the barn, the contrast between the bright sunshine outside and the shadows inside prevented her from seeing Philip, but she could hear the jangle of the stirrups as he unbuckled them from the gelding.

Since they'd lost the horse stalls when he'd chopped up the wood for fuel, he stood out in the open haymow. At her appearance, he paused only a second before continuing with taking off the saddle. "You didn't get enough of me earlier and had to come out and pounce on me again?"

His voice was light and teasing, but the topic was anything but those things. She couldn't make herself banter about it, not even if she tried.

She guided her horse to where the second horse stall used to stand, and she tied the lead line to a remaining hook in the wall.

"I take it we have company?" He lifted the saddle off the gelding.

She did the same. As they each groomed the horses, she told him about Serena and Tate and how she'd hired the young woman to help take care of Mr. Keller. For a short while, they conversed normally, as if nothing had happened between them earlier in the day, as if they hadn't shared the life-altering kiss and heated passion, and as if Weston hadn't seen it all.

Finally, as she hung up the bristly brush and Philip leaned the pitchfork against the wall after replenishing the troughs, she leveled a look at him past the two horses. "We need to talk."

One of his brows quirked. "And what have we been doing so far? Giving each other the silent treatment?"

She pressed her hands onto her hips, mostly to stop them from trembling. "We have to talk about what happened earlier today."

"What happened?"

"You know."

"Why don't you demonstrate again to remind me."

"Stop."

His grin made an appearance, and the light danced in his eyes, making him as handsome and appealing as always. Oh, dear heavens. Why did his smile have to be so devastating, almost seductive? Because suddenly, in watching his mouth, she couldn't think of anything else but how his lips had felt against hers earlier. And indeed, they'd been against hers in the most intimate of ways— hard and hot and heavy.

Her stomach quivered with the need to feel his lips that way again.

"I won't object if you want to do it all again." His voice dropped a notch, and his eyes also dropped to her mouth.

Yes, she'd demonstrate in a heartbeat, but she had to stay strong, couldn't give in to the desire . . . at least, not until she clarified the nature of their relationship and his intentions toward her.

Her mind scrambled to find the right words to say, the right words to tell him how she felt, the right words to ask him to be with her.

Even though he didn't take a step toward her, she could sense a shift in his mood, that he was finally growing more serious, that he wanted to say something too. Except that from the wrinkle of determination that was beginning to form in his brow, she suspected she might not like what he had to say.

"Philip . . ." She forced out his name, but the rest of her words clogged at the back of her throat like a logjam on the creek.

"Felicity, I've made plans to go. I have to."

No. The silent word screamed inside of her.

"It's the only way—"

"I love you." The words pushed past all the obstructions—the only words that could truly encapsulate all that he meant to her, all that she wanted, and all that he needed to know before he finalized his plans.

17

Had he heard her correctly? Surely she hadn't just said what he thought she had.

But from the way she was watching him, her brown eyes wide and vulnerable—and oh so beautiful—he knew he hadn't misunderstood.

Felicity loved him. She'd not only spoken the words, but her gaze was filled with her love.

He didn't merit it, not when he'd been such a scoundrel earlier today in taking advantage of her and kissing her. He deserved her wrath and disdain more than anything else.

"I vowed to myself that I wouldn't let another man kiss me unless I knew that he was the one I wanted to be with." She hugged her arms across her chest as if suddenly cold. "And you're the one I want to be with."

He swiped off his hat and jabbed his hand into his hair. This conversation was rapidly changing from bad to worse. How could he say anything in response to her revelations without hurting her completely?

That was exactly what he'd been afraid of all along—why he'd tried to leave Fairplay, why he'd been hesitant about getting too close to her. And now it had happened. She'd declared her love and all but proposed marriage.

Everything within him wanted to grab her into his arms and tell her she was the one he wanted to be with too. He could no longer deny that, even though he'd been trying so hard.

When he'd ridden into town earlier, he'd seriously considered again the possibility of sending Gustaf a notice that he wanted to cut his ties with the royal family. His blood had been heated, his body still on fire, and his heart filled with need for only Felicity. He'd realized that all he really wanted and all that truly mattered was her.

But when he'd arrived in town, a telegram had awaited him. Although anonymous, Philip had known it was from the prime minister. All it had said was: *The end is near.*

Of course, he'd burned the slip of paper. But the words had burned in his chest ever since. The end was near. A battle might be going on at this very moment in Lapland, and he wouldn't have word yet.

And if Gustaf were overthrown by rioters and rebels, and parliament called Philip home, what would he do then? He wouldn't be able to deny them. Not after they'd made so concerted an effort to oust Gustaf. Not after men had fought and possibly lost their lives for the cause of freedom and to have a monarch who submitted to the government instead of trying to do away with it.

Philip pressed his fingers to his throbbing temples and avoided looking at Felicity. The simple truth was that he couldn't walk away from his country and his duties. Not after doing his best over the past months to stay alive and avoid the assassin. And he couldn't promise Felicity a future with him in Lapland, especially since he didn't know what awaited him. His life, his future, his purpose—all of it was still so uncertain.

And then there was the constant threat of danger . . .

He'd seen a shadowy figure lounging in the hotel doorway across from the post office. The bulky shape of the body, broad shoulders, and square face had been similar to the man who'd been trailing him before. And although Philip hadn't been able to see the man's face, his skin had prickled with the realization that someone knew where he was.

Ever since that moment, the urgency inside had been mounting. He needed to leave Fairplay and take the peril far from Felicity.

But according to Mr. McLaughlin, the fellow who ran the livery and kept track of the stagecoach schedule, there probably wouldn't be any more stagecoaches or teamsters coming and going over the high mountain passes anytime soon, maybe not even until spring.

If he wanted to get to Denver, he'd have to brave the passes on a horse with as much of his belongings as he could carry on his saddle. Even then, Mr. McLaughlin recommended waiting a few more days to give the snow a chance to melt.

"Well . . .?" Felicity's voice hinted at hurt.

"I don't know what to say." He couldn't tell her he loved her in response. He had no right to utter such a declaration. Not now, when he wasn't in a position to offer her anything but trouble.

Her eyes glinted. Were they filling with tears?

He loathed himself for upsetting her.

"Your not knowing what to say speaks clearly enough." She spun and stalked toward the barn door.

He couldn't let her walk away like this. He had to try to make things a little better. But how?

His thoughts tumbled about like a ship in a storm, his stomach roiling. Was it finally time to tell her the truth about his situation? If he did so, surely she'd understand his choice to go wasn't an easy one.

"Felicity, wait."

She didn't slow her steps.

He stalked after her, needing to stop her before she exited and they lost the privacy of the moment. His long legs easily caught up to her, and he grabbed her arm, bringing her to a halt.

Without turning to face him, she sniffled.

She *was* crying.

Self-loathing stirred in him again. "I'm sorry—"

"Don't apologize. I don't want to hear it." She wrenched to free herself from him.

He held her fast. "I wish I could throw away my future and my responsibilities and stay here with you. I really do. But I can't . . . because . . ."

Did he really dare tell her? He hadn't told anyone else during his entire trip. And neither had Declan.

But what harm could come of revealing his identity now? While they were alone. When he was getting ready to leave.

"I don't want to hear your excuses, Philip." Her voice wobbled. "Please, just let me go." She reached up and swiped at her cheek, brushing away a tear.

"It's not really an excuse." He wanted to lighten the moment, wished he could make her smile. But maybe she'd forgive him more quickly if she knew the truth. He took a deep breath and then let the words rush out. "I'm a prince."

She stilled, but she didn't turn.

Just in case his first statement hadn't been clear enough, he said it again. "I'm Prince Carl Philip Glucksberg, second son of Gustaf Albert Glucksberg, the sovereign of the nation of Lapland." Actually the *former* sovereign.

This time she did spin, and her eyes were wide.

He loosened his hold on her arm but couldn't make himself let go of her. What was she feeling at his revelation? Curiosity? Awe? Respect?

He'd grown up with those kinds of reactions whenever he was in a new country where people didn't recognize him. Whenever he or one of his friends spoke up about his royalty, the nature of every relationship changed. People always treated him differently because of his royal status, and he'd never liked that.

Hopefully his relationship with Felicity wouldn't change. He didn't want to lose the easy way they interacted together.

"You're a prince?" She seemed to find her tongue and gave him a once-over as if that would solve this new riddle. When she tugged free of his hold and stepped back, he didn't go after her.

"Yes, I give you my word."

"Your word?" Her eyes narrowed. "If you really are a prince, then you've been lying to me about who you are all this time. So what value is your word?"

"My word is still solid—"

"How can I trust anything you say now?"

This wasn't the reaction he'd been expecting—certainly wasn't one he'd ever gotten before. Then again, nothing about Felicity was like anything he'd ever known.

"You lied to me." She crossed her arms as if daring

him to defy her.

"I didn't set out to deceive you. I simply withheld that piece of information."

"That's lying by omission, and it's still lying."

"But it wasn't intentional."

"So you were planning to leave without telling me the truth."

"I haven't told anyone during my travels. Only Declan knows. And I need it to stay that way."

Her eyelashes were still damp from when he'd made her cry a few minutes ago. But her eyes had begun to flash . . . with anger. "I'm not just anyone, Philip."

"I realize that."

"You should have trusted me."

"I do trust you."

"Then why didn't you say something sooner?"

He shrugged. "My situation is complicated and dangerous. My brother, who is now king of Lapland, wants me dead, has hired an assassin, and I don't want to put you in harm's way by association with me."

"Don't you think I can handle complicated and dangerous?"

What could he say to that? She was a strong woman and wasn't afraid of many things. She was capable of handling much responsibility—had proven it by taking on the management of the boardinghouse by herself as well as caring for the Kellers and now a new boarder. So what had prevented him from saying something about his identity sooner? She deserved the truth from him.

But as much as he wanted to give her a truthful answer, he couldn't pinpoint why he'd held back. "I don't know, Felicity. I guess I always planned on leaving, didn't think we'd ever see each other again once I was gone."

"The attraction between us? It means nothing to you?" Her voice dipped low and was again tinged with hurt.

"It does mean something—"

"Just not enough to have an honest conversation about whether there's any chance of us being together."

"That's not fair." Frustration began to nag him.

She watched him for a moment, clearly waiting for him to have that honest conversation now.

He sighed. "The truth is that I don't know if I'll live until tomorrow or next week. And so I haven't been able to plan my future."

"If the future is so uncertain, then shouldn't we make the most of every day that we have left?" Her tone took on a pleading note. "Why waste another moment?"

Was she right? "It's not as easy as that for me. With the unrest in my country, it's possible I may someday assume the role of king."

The afternoon sunshine slanted through the barn door, and it cascaded over her, highlighting the striking color of her hair, turning it a burnished copper. It contrasted her pale skin and enriched the brown of her eyes. She was exquisite, like the rarest of precious jewels.

The light also made the turmoil in her eyes all too clear. "So you're not necessarily rejecting me because of the danger. You're doing so because you're not sure if I'll fit in with your life if you become king."

"The law requires a prince to marry whomever parliament chooses."

Her shoulders deflated, and a coolness began to creep into her expression.

Had he just agreed that he was rejecting her? Because he wasn't. "Wait, that didn't come out right—"

"It came out loud and clear enough for me." Her tone was clipped. "All along, I knew you planned on leaving. I was the fool to ever believe you'd change your mind, that maybe I was more than a diversion."

"And you were—"

"I should have known I was nothing more than a poor girl with a poor background who could never be good enough for you."

She spun on her heels, and before he could say anything else or block her path, she stalked out of the barn.

He started after her, a strange desperation settling inside. But at the sound of a wagon slogging to a stop in the yard, he guessed his ride had arrived—the wagon from the livery that he'd arranged to come pick him up and drive him to town so that he wouldn't have to impose on Felicity any longer.

He couldn't follow her outside and finish the conversation in public. Instead, he had half a mind to chase after her and drag her back into the barn and tell her to forget everything he'd said, to forget any worries about the future, that all he wanted was the present moment with her.

If he were truly free to choose what he wanted for the future, to chart his own course, he suspected his decision would be easy. He would stop trying to make himself leave Felicity and would give in to the need to stay with her forever.

But the fact was, he wasn't free to decide his own future or pick his own wife. If he suggested Felicity, what advantage would she have that he could leverage? He'd have to find a way to present her to parliament so that they would find favor with her.

And if they told him no?

He shuddered to think of how disappointed he would be. And if she felt rejected and hurt now, the rejection and hurt then would only be worse. He couldn't do that to her. Couldn't put her through such pain.

With a half groan of frustration, he combed his fingers roughly through his hair before slamming his hat back down.

As difficult as this moment was, he had to stick with

his original plan to leave and sever the ties. It would be best for both of them if he didn't prolong the moment any longer.

18

Philip was gone. Good riddance.

Felicity scrubbed his shirt over the corrugated washboard, letting the force pummel the garment the way she wanted to pummel him. When she'd been cleaning his room, she'd found the discarded shirt tangled in his bedsheets.

Now, while outside laundering sheets and towels and a week's worth of clothing that belonged to both her and the Kellers, she wasn't sure why she was taking the time with his shirt.

"I should burn it." She held up the offending object, a tailored white linen shirt he'd worn at times to dinner parties at Mrs. Bancroft's. She stretched it to arm's length and examined it for any spots that needed extra soap. A stab of pain in her chest brought swift sobs to her throat and the sting of tears to her eyes.

"No," she whispered fiercely. "I won't cry."

She hadn't cried when he'd packed his belongings yesterday. She hadn't cried when he'd ridden away in the wagon from the livery. And she hadn't cried when she'd spent the rest of the day with the Kellers and Serena and Tate without him. Even though she'd felt his absence keenly, she'd been too angry to mourn his going.

And she'd been too busy, first with a visit from Patience and her husband Spencer and his little girl Evangeline, who'd been worried about her during the storm.

Then she'd spent the remainder of the day rearranging bedrooms. With Serena's efficient help, they'd moved the Kellers' belongings into the room off the kitchen. They'd all agreed Mr. Keller should still spend parts of the day and evening in the front room, where he could enjoy everyone else's company.

Serena had helped Felicity clean the bedrooms, carry up her belongings, and get situated. The young woman had been hardworking and eager to help. Though Tate hardly let her out of his sight and clung to her skirt most of the time, he was well-behaved.

Of course, Philip had said goodbye to the Kellers before leaving, so the couple had known he would no longer be staying at the boardinghouse. Since his departure, thankfully, Mrs. Keller hadn't spoken about his absence, although Felicity had felt her inquisitive gaze upon her from time to time.

Felicity had held her emotions at bay . . . until she'd crawled into bed—the bed Philip had used during the times he'd actually slept. And then, with his pine and woodsmoke scent filling her nostrils and nothing left to fill her head but thoughts of him, the tears had come.

She hadn't wanted to cry over him, but the pain of losing him had invaded every part of her heart.

She straightened, pressed her fist into her lower back, and kneaded her sore muscles. The midday sunshine was warming her so that she'd begun to perspire, and the grass was soggy around the backyard where the snow had melted. All traces of the snow angels they'd made yesterday were gone, and only remnants of the drifts remained to show that there had been a storm.

"Why did I have to let myself care about someone who didn't love me in return?" Her question was swallowed up by the flapping of the sheets and garments she'd already washed that were blowing on the clothesline.

Philip's revelation that he was a prince had shocked her. But the more she'd thought about it, the more she'd been able to see the princely side to him—the regal way he'd held himself at times, the authority he wielded, and even a privileged outlook on life, as if the world was his for the taking.

Maybe she'd once aspired to better her station and improve herself, but she'd been put in her place often enough—especially most recently by Mrs. Bancroft—that she'd resigned herself to being a simple woman with a simple life.

But Philip wasn't simple. He wasn't merely a wealthy gentleman traveling at his leisure, and he wasn't just from a different country and culture. He was from a different world altogether—a world she'd never understand or aspire to. He was way beyond her. Untouchable, unreachable, and unattainable.

And now that she knew who he really was, she understood just how foolish she'd been to assume that they could ever be together. She'd made a complete idiot of herself professing her love, giving him everything within her, and telling him that she wanted to be with him when a relationship with a prince was impossible.

Of course, she wouldn't have allowed herself to get carried away if she'd known his identity. But he'd known. He'd still flirted with her endlessly, and he'd let her kiss him. He'd even hinted he wanted more with her. But in the end, he hadn't wanted her enough to love her in return.

He should have said something sooner or established better boundaries . . . Not that he hadn't tried to set boundaries. She'd sensed his restraint and his carefulness. Even so, he should have trusted her sooner and revealed who he really was. Maybe then they could have at least parted ways as friends.

"Why couldn't I be satisfied with a nice, normal man like Weston Oakley?" This time she spoke her question louder, unable to hold back the anger toward herself for being so foolish. "He would have loved me and married me."

At the clearing of a throat behind her, Felicity spun to find Serena and Tate standing only a few feet away. "I'm sorry." Serena cast her gaze downward as though she expected a chastisement.

Tate had fisted her skirt and was leaning into her, his eyes haunted.

As with every time Felicity interacted with the young mother and her son, she sensed that Serena's story was complicated and tragic. Maybe someday the woman would feel comfortable revealing it. But until then, Felicity would be patient.

"I'd like to finish the rest of the laundry for you." Serena nodded to the items that remained in a basket next to the washtub.

Philip's wet shirt still dripped from Felicity's hand, and she wanted to hide it behind her back, the evidence of how much she was missing him even though he'd been gone for less than twenty-four hours.

Was he already on his way to Denver? Or would he have to stay in town for a few more days?

Her sights locked on the Tarryall Mountain Range and Kenosha Pass in the east with their bright, snowy tops. They were still covered, likely too treacherous for travel. But if the warm temperatures continued, he might be able to find a way out of the high country soon.

He'd mentioned the danger that he was in, that his brother was trying to assassinate him. And although he hadn't specifically said so, she guessed that was why he'd taken a different name and was keeping his identity hidden—so that he could stay out of his brother's clutches. Maybe that was part of the reason he'd never stayed long in any one place during his travels and why he'd been anxious to leave South Park.

Serena picked up the bar of soap in the grass. "Will you show me how to do the laundry? I'd like to learn. Then you'll be free to ride into town on your errand."

Her errand. Felicity draped Philip's shirt over the nearest portion of clothesline, not bothering to pass it through the wringer. "Yes, I am running low on several pantry items." Although, she couldn't remember which ones. She certainly wasn't going into town simply to find out what had become of Philip. But while she was there, she could discreetly inquire about him, couldn't she?

After instructing Serena on how to use the washboard and the wringer, Felicity rushed inside to change and make herself more presentable for a trip into Fairplay. She chose her favorite emerald skirt and blouse and matching bonnet—but not for Philip's sake, and certainly not because he'd commented on how pretty she looked in it on several occasions.

Even so, as she rode through the thick mud and the many puddles into town and down Main Street, she hoped Philip would spot her and realize how much he liked her. Not that such an acknowledgement would do either of them any good. They would still go their separate ways. But at least he'd take the image of her at her best with him.

After parking and making her way down the boardwalk to Simpkins General Store, she tried not to be too obvious as she searched for a sign of Philip somewhere. Maybe he'd be inside the store reading the newspapers, as he so often had been over recent weeks.

What news had he been searching for? News of his homeland? Of his brother?

But as she entered the store and ordered her items, she didn't catch sight of him anywhere. Had he already left town?

"And how are the passes?" she asked Captain Jim, trying to keep her voice nonchalant. "Has anyone dared to traverse them yet?"

"No, Mr. Berg ain't left town yet." Captain Jim's loud voice carried through the store.

Felicity snorted. "Well, that's too bad." She tamped down her mortification at how easily the store owner had read her need for Philip. "I was hoping he was long gone by now."

"Don't think you're gonna get rid of that fella so easily." Captain Jim finished packaging the sugar she didn't really need. "Not when he's scared off every man from having you so that he can keep you for himself."

The store had grown silent—so silent Felicity guessed every patron could hear the wild thumping of her heart. "That's nonsense."

"Ain't nonsense at all. Had lots of fellas wanting to take that job you advertised for, but he warned every single one of them to stay away."

At the revelation, her stomach melted into a slushy puddle just like the snow. No doubt the store owner was exaggerating, but she soaked up the words about Philip like the earth soaking up the melting snow.

After paying and offering her thanks, she made small talk with several women, catching up on how everyone had weathered the storm. Mostly she was dallying to see if Philip would arrive. But after lingering longer than was respectable, she headed out and started down the boardwalk toward her wagon.

She wasn't ready for her time in town to be over. Maybe she should seek out her solicitor. Or perhaps she'd go to the bank and take out the money she'd need to pay Serena for her work.

"Miss Courtney?" At the call of her name from the walkway between two businesses, she paused. In the shadows of the snowy-muddy path stood a man wearing a cloak and flat black hat pulled low. He'd been in the store only moments ago—or at least she thought she'd glimpsed him.

"May I help you?" Had his voice contained a tinge of a foreign accent? An accent that sounded similar to Philip's?

"Philip has asked me to come and get you."

Yes, he did have an accent. Perhaps he was a companion traveling with Philip. More likely a servant, because a prince wouldn't travel without his manservant, would he?

"He'd like to speak a few more words with you," the man said. "If you're agreeable."

A few more words? Felicity's heart gave an extra beat. After having had all night and all day to think on their relationship, had Philip changed his mind about wanting to be with her?

"Come this way." The man waved his hand in the direction of the alley at the end of the walkway. "He's just around the corner."

Felicity took a step then hesitated. Something didn't feel quite right. About the man. About his claim that Philip was waiting.

"After you." He waved her ahead of him.

She took another step, then two, before stopping. "Tell Philip if he would like to talk, he can visit me at the boardinghouse."

Should she extend an invitation for dinner? Surely the Kellers would love to see him again.

The man glanced past her toward Main Street, then in the next instant, before she could move, he thrust a long, sharp knife against her chest.

She released a startled half scream.

At her slight sound, he dug the tip through her cloak, pricking her. "Don't make another sound. If you do, the next cut will be deeper."

She could feel the warmth of blood beginning to soak into her bodice. Suddenly she knew this stranger wasn't taking her to Philip. He had something much more sinister in mind.

His hand clamped about her arm, and he forced her toward the alley. As they rounded the corner, of course there was no sign of Philip. Instead, the fellow picked up his pace and thrust her toward a waiting horse and wagon.

Both fear and dread raced through her, and she began to drag her steps. She had to fight back now, couldn't go anywhere with this stranger. If she did, she might never return.

Before she could grab his arm and try to dodge the knife, he shoved something else at her—a rag with the stench of a chemical saturating it. He clamped it against her nose and mouth so that she could hardly breathe.

The world began to spin around her. Whatever was on the rag was making her weak and lightheaded. If she didn't get away from him, she was going to faint.

"Don't worry." The man's low voice taunted near her ear. "You'll get your reunion with Philip. Just not the way you planned."

Before she could make sense of his words, blackness hovered nearer. She fought against it, against her captor. But in the next instant, the world disappeared.

19

He couldn't go visit Felicity. Couldn't. Wouldn't.

Philip placed his camera box and tripod down on the bed of his hotel room along with the bag of all the other equipment. The afternoon of photographing at one of the local ranches had occupied his time but hadn't taken his mind off Felicity.

Nothing had taken his mind off her. Not since the moment he'd ridden away from the boardinghouse yesterday.

His stomach growled, reminding him he'd already skipped the noon meal and couldn't miss supper—not with the waft of chicken and dumplings rising from the dining room all the way to the second floor of Hotel Windsor.

Even though he still didn't feel like eating, he paced to the door. He needed sustenance, but he also didn't want anything or anyone but her. He paused with his hand on the doorknob.

"What am I doing?" The question slipped out and contained all the agony of losing her. Not only that, but he could still see the tears on her lashes, hear the pain in her voice, and see the hurt in her eyes when she'd said she'd never be good enough for him.

The truth was, *he'd* never be good enough for *her*. Not only was he a scoundrel for deceiving her about his identity, but she was pure and innocent and kindhearted in a way he'd never been. And she cared about others more than she cared about herself, while he was selfish.

He rubbed a hand down his mouth and chin to hold back the curses at himself. He had a duty to his country—one he wouldn't neglect. But he also had a duty to himself too, didn't he? Didn't he deserve some voice in his future and in his happiness?

The concept was difficult to fathom, especially after the many years he'd lived to please his father and country. He'd loved and admired his father, but the king had been a hard and demanding man and had shown little affection. Nevertheless, Philip had tried to be adequate and make his father proud.

Gustaf, on the other hand, had always resented their father and had surrounded himself with friends and advisors who stirred up doubts and arrogance. Gustaf's rebellious ways had only contributed to Philip's desire to be all the more compliant. He'd learned to be lighthearted to ease the tension and problems that arose with Gustaf and his parents.

In trying to make everyone else happy and smooth over the problems, had he lost the ability to look out for his own needs? Like the need to have the woman he loved?

He groaned and leaned his head against the door. Yes, he loved Felicity. He'd been trying to deny it all this time, but he'd started falling in love with her the first moment he'd laid eyes on her, when she'd taken the seat across the table from him at Mrs. Bancroft's and had responded to one of his flirtations with a sassy comment.

A rushing waterfall of need plummeted through his chest, nearly buckling him to his knees. He needed her in his life, couldn't imagine a future without her in it. In fact, he didn't want to go another day without seeing or talking to her.

Was there a way to pursue the woman he loved and still maintain duty to his country? He couldn't ride away from her without trying to find a solution—one in which he still obeyed the laws of his country regarding marriage but also had the option of negotiating with parliament.

Maybe it was time to stop trying to please everyone and once in a while stand up for something that was important to him. And she was important. She was the most important person in his life.

He straightened and pressed a fist against the ache in

his chest. He had to go tell her of his feelings, his love, his hope to find a way to be together, everything. He wasn't sure how anything could ever work out between them, since he couldn't abandon his country and she wouldn't abandon the boardinghouse. But even if they couldn't be together now, he wanted the assurance that someday they could be reunited.

If she'd still have him . . . He didn't deserve her love for riding away from her yesterday. But he'd do whatever he could to earn it back.

He threw open the door to his hotel room and stalked out, barely remembering to close the door behind him. Hope, anticipation, excitement made his steps light and quick as he raced down the stairway.

He'd ride out to the boardinghouse, fall onto his knees as dramatically as he could, and beg her to forgive him for being such an idiot. He'd do what he should have done yesterday—tell her he loved her and that he had for a long time. And then together, they'd discuss the future. So much was uncertain about what would happen in the days and weeks to come in Lapland, with his brother and the state of the kingship. But he wouldn't sacrifice having her. He couldn't.

With new energy and his hunger forgotten, he descended into the wide hallway. The haze of cigar smoke enveloped him in the dim light of the evening. Laughter and conversation and the clinking of dishes echoed from the dining room, filled with the mostly male population staying at the hotel.

Philip passed by without a glance, his focus on the door and the need to find a horse at the livery that he could use for riding out to the boardinghouse.

"Oh, Mr. Berg." Mr. Fehling's call came from the dining room.

Philip didn't slow his footsteps, didn't want to waste another minute—not even another second—in returning to Felicity and pleading with her. And even though Mr. Fehling was a kind hotel proprietor, he was quite the talker. Usually, Philip didn't mind and had spent many an evening with Declan and Mr. Fehling, smoking cigars and having lively discussions.

"Wait, Philip." Mr. Fehling's voice held a note of concern.

Philip halted in front of the door and turned just as the heavyset man lumbered into the hallway, his shiny forehead and receding hairline perspiring. He held a coffee pot in one hand, was rarely without it.

"I tried to catch your attention when you entered a little bit ago." Mr. Fehling began to dig in the front pocket of his stained apron. "But you ran up those stairs before I could manage a word."

"You'll have to excuse me, sir. I'm in a hurry tonight."

Mr. Fehling fished in his pocket a moment longer before pulling out a folded paper. "Some fella stopped by and insisted I give this to you. Said it was urgent, that you'd want it tonight."

Urgent? Philip's pattering pulse tripped over itself. "What's the urgency? Has something happened to Felicity?"

"Sorry, Mr. Berg." Mr. Fehling handed him the slip with a sheepish smile. "I admit, I tried reading it, but the message is written in a foreign language."

"Probably Danish, my natural tongue." Philip took the paper with a growing anticipation. What if it was the news he'd been waiting for from the prime minister? So far, all their communication had been private and secretive. But if the prime minister was being open with their exchanges, then that had to mean the rebellion was over and Gustaf was out of power.

He slipped open the half sheet to find a brief, neatly penned note in Danish: *I have her. If you want to save her, you must hand yourself over to me at the abandoned Hawthorne Mine. Alone.*

"No." The whisper came out strangled, and his blood turned to ice. He didn't need an explanation to know the note was referring to Felicity. And he also didn't need an explanation to know the note was from the assassin who'd been trailing him during his travels.

This was his worst nightmare coming true.

As the horror spread through him, he tried to clear his mind so that he could think. He had to do something to save her. Had to find a way to free her without bringing her more harm.

At the prospect of her suffering in any way, his gut churned with the need to be sick.

"What's wrong, Mr. Berg?" Mr. Fehling took a step toward him, concern etching his forehead. "Bad news?"

Philip nodded. The note said he had to go alone. But should he at least tell Mr. Fehling about the kidnapping? Maybe the local sheriff? What was unclear was why the assassin hadn't just taken him prisoner and had instead captured Felicity to use as ransom.

He had no guarantee that, even if he handed himself over, the killer would set Felicity free. What would stop the assassin from doing away with them both?

"I have to go and take care of something." Philip peered past the dusty window at the front of the hotel. He didn't know how far Hawthorne Mine was from Fairplay, but he'd heard it was abandoned and guessed it was several miles to the west in the foothills. The evening sky was already turning dark. By the time he reached the mine, night would have settled, making his rescue of Felicity all that much more dangerous.

The fear and desperation inside prodded him to leave. Who knew how much time he'd already let elapse since the assassin had left the note? And who knew what he'd done to Felicity by now?

Yet as much as Philip wanted to rush out and try to

rescue her, he suspected the assassin was laying a trap for him and that he had to move cautiously or he wouldn't be able to help Felicity. Before leaving, he had to find out more about Hawthorne Mine. Then he'd have an easier time navigating once he got there. "Mr. Fehling, you know most of the men in Fairplay and in the surrounding area, don't you?"

"Do I?" His voice rose with a note of pride. "Of course I do. I've lived here longer than almost anyone else and know everyone."

"Then maybe you can help me. I need to speak to any miners who may have once worked at the old, abandoned Hawthorne Mine."

Mr. Fehling, still holding his pot of coffee, pressed a hand to his chin, squishing his flesh as he stared straight ahead, deep in thought.

After a moment, he released his chin and snapped his fingers. "I know of two fellas. One lives in town and the other works as a cowhand at Updegraff Ranch." The hotel proprietor gave Philip their names and where to look for them at this time of the night, indicating that one or both would be at the taverns in town.

With his heart thudding with urgent need, Philip crossed to the door. He wasn't sure how he'd find Felicity and free her, but all he knew was that he had to do something—that he couldn't let her get in the middle of this war with his brother.

As he exited, he nodded his thanks to Mr. Fehling. "If I'm not back at the hotel within two hours, send the sheriff out to find me at Hawthorne Mine."

He'd probably be dead. But he prayed that at the very least, Felicity would be alive and safe.

20

Felicity awoke with a pounding headache. As she drew in a breath of musty air, her eyes flew open, and she found herself in a cavern of some sort, lit by a lantern placed on a rocky ledge above her. The light illuminated a low granite ceiling and rough walls on either side. Ahead, steel tracks led down a long passageway that disappeared into darkness. On her opposite side, the metal tracks ran to another black chasm.

Where was she? A mine?

At the trickle of water behind her, she shifted to find thin threads of water running down the wall and forming a narrow creek beside the tracks.

She had to be in a mine. What other place could it be? But why was she here?

Her thoughts raced back to the trip she'd made to town out of her need to see Philip again. In her last waking moments after she'd walked out of the store, what had happened? Had someone really threatened her with a knife and then forced her to walk toward a wagon?

Yes, there had been a man with a foreign accent. At first, she'd assumed he was someone with Philip. But she'd clearly been wrong. The man's intentions toward Philip were less than honorable.

Was he the assassin Philip had mentioned? The one his brother had sent after him? If so, what was he doing with her?

She didn't have to think long to figure that out. In fact, she didn't need any time. If the assassin had been in the General Store and had heard Captain Jim blathering on about how much Philip liked her, the man had probably captured her to lure Philip down into the mine after her.

Once Philip was here in the mine, the assassin would be able to trap him and kill him.

Even if Philip didn't love her and didn't want to be with her, he was too noble and caring not to come after her once he learned of her plight. He wasn't the sort of man who would leave her to rot while he left town and saved himself . . . unfortunately . . .

She really wished at this moment that he was that sort of man and wouldn't attempt to rescue her. But she expected that as soon as he got news the assassin had her, he'd rush out and put himself into life-threatening danger to help her.

In fact, he was probably already on his way.

She glanced around again. The assassin wasn't anywhere in sight. But that didn't mean he wasn't lurking somewhere nearby.

She tugged on her arms, which were bound behind her at the wrists. Then she tried to move her legs only to find that they, too, were tied tightly together. At least her mouth wasn't gagged.

But maybe that was intentional. Maybe once Philip arrived and started calling for her, the assassin hoped she'd respond, drawing him toward her.

Obviously, as an assassin, he would be a trained and experienced killer. He wouldn't leave room for any mistakes and had probably plotted out every detail.

Except that he didn't know her. He didn't know how much she loved Philip. And he didn't know what lengths she'd go to in order to protect him.

She was no damsel in distress. She was a strong woman who could do whatever she set her mind to. And that meant her first order of business was to free herself from her binding. If she wasn't lying there tied up and helpless when Philip arrived, then the assassin wouldn't be able to lure him in and kill him.

She dug her fingers into the gravel behind her. Surely with a sharp rock she could saw through her binding. If she did so quietly enough, maybe the assassin wouldn't find out.

With nothing sharp enough beneath her, she inched down the track. Her fingers connected with a lone rusty nail, and for a short while she rubbed it against the rope, but at the odd angle, she didn't make much progress.

As a sense of urgency settled inside her, she wiggled farther from her original spot, combing the gravel as she went. To her side, her gaze snagged on a section of the tracks where the metal had been torn away, leaving a gap . . . and a jagged edge.

She rapidly positioned her wrists and the rope over the knifelike fragment of metal and began to saw.

The metal sliced into her arm, and she sucked in a breath at the pain that raced up her flesh. With blood running down her arm and onto her wrists, her skin grew slick, but she continued to slice at the rope, this time sawing slowly and meticulously, knowing she could hurt herself badly if she weren't careful.

When the rope was frayed almost to the end, she wrestled the final part until it snapped. With her hands free, she examined her cut. It was deep and still bleeding profusely. As quietly as she could, she ripped part of her petticoat, tied it around the wound, then began working on freeing her feet.

She wasn't sure how much time had elapsed during her efforts to cut herself free. But she guessed the assassin would be checking on her again soon. She had to position herself where he'd left her and wrap the rope back around her feet so that she still appeared to be bound.

As she began to scramble toward the area where she'd first awoken, she stopped short at the sight of blood covering the gravel near the broken rail. She'd obviously bled all over everything, and if the assassin came near enough, he'd notice the blood. He'd be too proficient to miss it.

She dragged her fingers across the gravel, trying to cover the spots. Her clean-up job wasn't perfect, but she'd have to pray that in the low lighting of the tunnel, the assassin wouldn't notice anything.

At the crunch of footsteps and a light that seemed to be coming from a nearby cross tunnel, she lay down the way she'd been when she'd awoken, wrapped the rope around her ankles as tightly as possible, then slipped her hands behind her back out of sight. With her eyes closed, she pretended to be asleep, breathing slowly and rhythmically.

Even with her eyes closed, she could sense the brightening of the tunnel when the newcomer stepped into it. He seemed to be holding the lantern up and was likely examining her.

Anger wrestled around her insides more than fear—anger that Philip's brother was trying to kill him, anger that he'd had to run for his life, anger that after surviving this long he was in danger because of her.

No, she wouldn't let anything happen to him tonight.

Letting her anger fuel her, she put on the best performance she could. She prayed she looked as innocent and gullible as she had when he'd first approached her. She needed to convince him that she wasn't a threat, that he had nothing to fear from her.

But the truth was, he had everything to fear, because she intended to protect the man she loved, even if she had to put herself in danger to do so.

She still loved Philip and probably always would. But she was beginning to understand why he'd always been making plans to leave Fairplay, why he'd sometimes even seemed in a hurry to go. Because he'd been dodging danger and hadn't wanted to bring her—or anyone else near him—into the turmoil of his life.

Well, once they were both free of the assassin—yes, she was being like her sister Charity and thinking optimistically in the situation—she wouldn't try to convince Philip to stay. Wouldn't even encourage it. Instead, she'd push him out of town and on his way just as soon as he could go so that he'd stay out of reach of his brother.

Would he have to keep running and hiding his whole life?

Poor Philip. What a lonely and dangerous existence that would be.

Her captor assessed her and the passageway for several long seconds. Then the light began to fade with the retreating footsteps. Even after he was gone, she waited, unmoving.

Finally she pushed up, took her bindings off, and stood. She guessed the assassin was keeping an eye on the entrance, lying in wait for Philip to make an appearance.

She'd never be able to sneak past him and leave the mine. Her only other option was to hide.

She turned and assessed the tunnel first one way and then the other.

The far end of the tunnel didn't seem quite as dark. Was that the direction of the entrance? Perhaps radiance from the moon and stars was brightening it. That made sense. If Philip entered there, he'd see her on the track and come rushing toward her only to have the assassin step out of the side tunnel and block him.

She'd have to go the opposite way.

She didn't know much about mines, but from the cobwebs and dust and broken rail, she guessed the area she was in was no longer in use. More likely, the entire mine was old and abandoned. If she started wandering around, she might encounter old tunnels that could cave in, loose rocks or beams, even unmarked shafts that she could fall into.

She would have to be careful, but she could do it. For Philip. If she wasn't lying there tied up and helpless when Philip arrived, then the assassin wouldn't be able to lure him in and kill him.

Creeping forward as silently as possible, she started down the track toward the unknown. As she reached the dark edges, she slowed her steps.

At a sound behind her, she glanced over her shoulder to find that the man with the flat black hat and cloak had stepped out of his hiding spot again. He looked at the empty spot where she'd been and then cursed. Even though the profanity was in a different language, it was still clear enough.

She darted forward, and her pulse sped with the need to get away and disappear into the darkness before he noticed her.

More cursing sounded behind her.

She picked up her pace.

A second later, he shouted, the call following her.

He'd spotted her.

With an urgency born of desperation, she raced faster, praying she could either outrun him or find a place to hide before he caught her.

21

At a distant bang, Philip's body tensed.

Was it the crash of rocks or mining tools? Hopefully it wasn't the shot of a gun. Please, not a gun.

Philip tried to crawl faster on his hands and knees, but he had to crouch low, his broad shoulders scraping the sides of the tunnel and slowing him down.

The fellow he'd spoken to in town had assured him the back entrance would lead into the main drifts. But so far, after crawling for at least a hundred feet, he hadn't come across any other passageways.

He maneuvered the lantern ahead of him, the flame low to avoid drawing attention until he was close enough to Felicity to protect her.

He'd considered going in without light, but the old miner had indicated that he would get lost without it. Additionally, with the light he could read the map the fellow had drawn for him, showing him how to cross over to the front entrance of the mine.

The assassin was likely waiting by the main mine opening with Felicity, someplace where Philip would see her and be unable to resist going in after her.

Obviously the assassin had been in Fairplay for some time, at least since before the storm had closed the passes. He could have struck earlier. Could have attempted to capture him instead of Felicity. Could have slipped into his hotel room at night and slit his throat.

So why hadn't the killer done any of those things? Philip hadn't been able to work out the answers during the ride to the mine. Instead, panic had been building so that now it had developed not only a home but an entire city inside him.

Maybe he should have gone to the sheriff right away and rounded up a group to rescue Felicity instead of coming alone. He'd just been too afraid that if he showed up with help, the assassin would carry through on his threat to harm Felicity. And Philip couldn't take the chance of anything else bad happening to her. This was already terrible enough.

With a huff of frustration, he wormed his way forward. He had to hurry and reach Felicity before the assassin grew tired of waiting for him to arrive and began to suspect that he was up to something.

Gradually the ceiling began to rise, and soon he was able to walk hunched over. The way was fairly clear with a rock pile or two he had to navigate around, just as the old miner had warned.

At another bang, this time closer, he halted. The sound was most definitely a gunshot.

What could it mean? Was the assassin shooting at someone?

His heart thudded with a burst of alarm at the prospect of the gunshots being fired at Felicity.

The lantern light cast a glow ahead on what appeared to be an intersecting tunnel. Philip held up the map and tried to determine his location. Was this the tunnel he needed to turn into so that he could make his way toward the main entrance?

The slap of footsteps was drawing closer from the intersecting tunnel. He set the lantern down, stuffed the map into his shirt, and unholstered his revolver. Then he flattened himself against the wall, the ceiling finally high enough that he didn't have to slouch so far.

A figure raced into the intersection of the two tunnels. He had only to glimpse the hair to know it was Felicity. Before she could run to the other side, he snaked out his arm and caught hold of her, dragging her out of the line of the assassin's fire.

She gasped and might have screamed, but he cupped a hand over her mouth and in the same motion drew her against him.

"It's me," he whispered.

In the middle of struggling, she froze. Her eyes widened.

At the oncoming footsteps, he released her, pushed her behind him, and lifted his gun.

She sidled behind him near his back. Her breathing was labored. From the blood stains on her coat, she'd clearly sustained injuries.

He didn't have time to question her. He had to stop her pursuer.

Drawing in a steadying breath, he peeked around the corner. A man was about fifty feet away, his frame difficult to see in the darkness. Even so, Philip pointed his revolver and took a shot.

The footsteps halted, a gunshot resounded in return, and an instant later a bullet whizzed past him.

He pushed Felicity away from him down the passageway he'd just traversed. "Go. There's a back way in and out of the mine."

Felicity didn't budge but clutched his coat. "I'm not leaving without you."

"Do it." He didn't care that his voice was harsh.

"No." Her whisper was stubborn.

He peeked around the corner again. The assassin wasn't in sight. Where had he gone?

Philip pulled back. Could they make a run for the exit? How far would they get before the assassin was on their trail? They would be out in the open with no place to hide.

He had to at least make Felicity leave. Then he could battle it out with the assassin.

His revolver held six rounds. Now that he'd fired one, he only had five left. And of course, he hadn't taken the time to go back to his room for more cartridges.

The assassin likely had more than one gun, extra ammunition, and a cache of other weapons to use against him. And no doubt he was a skilled and experienced fighter, so that even in hand-to-hand combat, Philip wouldn't stand a chance.

"You get a head start," Philip whispered, trying for another tactic with Felicity. "Take my horse and ride back to town and bring out help." He had to get her to go on without him so that she made it out. Even if he didn't, at least he'd be able to die in peace knowing she got away.

He could feel her loosen her hold on his coat, as if she was considering his proposition.

Slowly, cautiously, he started to poke his head out to gauge where the assassin had gone. But as soon as he did, a gunshot fired, and he jerked back as a bullet pinged against the tunnel wall near his head.

With only his lantern giving off faint light, he darted a glance to see the assassin in what appeared to be an alcove of some sort—one that was several dozen paces away. Not far.

Philip took aim and shot again. But the assassin was clearly skilled and dropped out of sight before the bullet could get near him.

"Please, Felicity." He didn't care that his whisper sounded desperate or that he was begging her. He needed her to go before it was too late.

"I won't make it back to town in time," she whispered. "We have to think of another way to outsmart him."

"There is no other way." He guessed he could hold out in this standoff for a short while. But what then? "You have to go. Now."

"Give yourself up, Your Highness," the voice called in Danish. "If you hand yourself over willingly, I shall allow the young woman to go."

Philip knew he shouldn't contemplate doing as the man asked, but what other choice did he have?

"What did he say?" Felicity whispered.

Philip didn't want to tell her. She'd only protest.

"Do you give me your word that you'll leave her unharmed?" Philip responded in Danish, not wanting Felicity to be part of his negotiations.

"I vow it," came the reply. "She was only a means to draw you here."

As before, Philip didn't understand why the assassin was going to such trouble to bring him to the mine when he could have killed him someplace else.

She nudged him from behind. "What's happening?"

"I'm giving myself over to him."

"You can't." This time her whisper was harsh. "I won't let you."

"It's too late. I've already agreed to it so long as he allows you to leave."

She started to tug him backward. "We'll make a run for it together."

He resisted her pull. "It's too dangerous. The tunnel has no place to take cover."

"At least you'll have a chance to escape and possibly live."

"He'll shoot me in the back and then kill you next. If I turn myself in, at least I can guarantee that the woman I love will live."

"Love?" Her whisper rose with disbelief.

He hadn't meant to make his declaration of love to her in the bowels of the mine with an assassin shooting at them from around the corner. But if he didn't make it out of the mine alive, now she would know the truth. "I was a fool not to tell you yesterday. Because the truth is, I love you more than my own life."

"Hand yourself over, Your Highness," the assassin called again in Danish. "It's the only way."

"I'm saying goodbye," Philip whispered to her. At least, that was what he was trying to do.

In the low lantern light, he studied her face one last time. Even with her face streaked with dirt and her hair tangled with cobwebs, she took his breath away.

"I won't let you do it." Tears welled up in her beautiful eyes.

Before he could talk himself out of it, he bent down and captured her lips. He took her with a passionate force—one that didn't hold anything back but contained every ounce of his love so that she would know with certainty he loved her more than anything or anyone.

She responded with desperation, pressing into him, meeting his kiss and giving back to him in the same measure, her mouth melding and mingling and telling him that she loved him in return.

As he started to pull away, she clung to him. "Please," she whispered against his lips. "Please don't leave me."

He didn't want to be apart from her. In fact, if by some miracle he survived the assassin's scheming, he wouldn't let Felicity out of his sight ever again.

"Take this and be safe." He thrust his revolver into her hand. Then before she could stop him, he released her, broke away, and stepped into the intersection so that the assassin could see him.

"No!" Her cry echoed in the hollow tunnel, but thankfully she didn't follow him.

"Go, Felicity. Go now!"

Tears began coursing down her cheeks as she took a step away.

He let himself take one last look before facing the assassin who'd slipped out of the alcove where he'd been hiding, his gun aimed at Philip's heart.

"You vowed you would let her go." Philip held up his hands to show that he was no longer armed.

"She means nothing to me." The fellow was donned in a simple cloak and a black felt hat and approached cautiously.

She meant everything to Philip. From the corner of his eyes, he could see her slowly creeping backward away from him. He wanted her to run, to get as far away as possible before the assassin killed him. Not only did he want to keep her from witnessing the deed, but he also wanted her to be well out of harm's way, just in case the assassin changed his mind.

Could he distract, possibly delay, the assassin and give her more time?

"Take me someplace else to kill me." It was the only thing he could think of. "I don't want Felicity to see me dying."

The assassin was closing in on him, his gun unswerving. "Now that you have handed yourself over to me, I cannot risk you getting away. Not after how long I have been hunting you."

Hunting. The word sent a chill up Philip's spine. "Why bring me here to the mine? Why not kill me on the streets of Fairplay?"

"You have been too closely guarded. But here, with the woman you love at risk, you will do as I say, even if your guard tries to rescue you."

His guard? Maybe he had a bodyguard after all, watching out for him and keeping him safe. But what could the bodyguard do now to stop him from giving his life to save Felicity's? Nothing. And the assassin knew it.

The fellow stopped a foot away and rammed the barrel of the revolver into Philip's forehead.

Up so close, he could finally see the man's features. He was stocky and clean-shaven and looked like an average fellow on the street. Perhaps that was intentional so that he'd be able to blend in and sneak up on his prey. The only thing about him that was unnatural was the deadly glint in his eyes, as if he was taking pleasure in this moment right before the kill.

"Have you any last words you would like me to deliver to the king?"

"Tell him that I forgive him." In spite of everything, Philip couldn't take bitterness and unforgiveness with him to the grave. "And tell him to be a good king."

"He already is a good king." The assassin settled his finger on the trigger. "And now he will be even better without a usurper in his way."

At the click of the hammer, Philip closed his eyes and waited for the blast that would tear through him and end his life. Strangely, he wasn't afraid. The only thing he regretted was that Felicity would have to witness this crime. It would be a terrible memory that she would have for a long time. He hoped eventually she would recover and go on to find love with another man.

In the next instant a gun blasted, followed by a second blast, and Philip waited for the pain and then the oblivion.

But nothing happened . . . except for silence. Was he already in paradise? If so, why was the air still musty and cold? And why could he hear the trickle of water running off the walls?

The assassin's barrel was no longer against his head.

Philip cracked open an eye to find that the fellow had taken a step back. He was holding his shooting arm, and the sleeve of his coat was turning dark with blood beneath his fingers. His eyes were wide and unseeing. And he wavered, as if he was about to topple over.

Had Felicity shot him?

Philip turned to find Felicity only ten feet away with his revolver pointed at the assassin. She glanced from the gun to the wound and then back, and her hand began to shake. Even so, she didn't lower the weapon but kept it aimed at the assassin.

Was there a chance he and Felicity could escape now while the assassin was wounded?

With a surge of renewed energy, Philip grabbed the assassin's arm and banged it against the wall. The revolver slipped from the man's grip and clattered to the ground.

Philip swiped it up and then pointed it at the fellow.

But before he could pull the trigger and disable the assassin even further, the man wavered again, fell forward, and landed face-first on the ground, with a bullet hole in the back of his head.

Where had that shot come from? Certainly not Felicity. She hadn't been at an angle to do that. And the shot was too precise, the work of someone who was an excellent marksman.

Philip peered down the passageway to find a shadowy figure lurking in an alcove, his gun out and pointed his way. By the bulky body, hefty shoulders, and square face, Philip recognized him as the man he'd seen trailing him from time to time, giving him the prickles of unease.

Rapidly, Philip shifted his revolver and aimed it at the newcomer. "Don't come any closer or I'll shoot."

22

She'd shot and injured a man.

Unable to control her shaking, Felicity stared at the assassin lying on the ground. She'd injured his arm holding out the gun, intending to disable him. And she had.

But someone else had followed them into the tunnels and had been the one to kill him.

In front of her, Philip raised his gun, then peeked out into the passageway, just as he had before with the other man.

Felicity drew in a taut breath. Was another assassin on Philip's trail? Would the danger never end?

If they ever got free from the mine and the threats, she resolved again to send Philip far away from Fairplay. He had to hide in another town someplace new where he could be safe for a little while.

She only had to picture the assassin with the gun

pointed against Philip's forehead to feel a fresh surge of resolve. Even though she'd been trying to escape the way Philip had wanted, she hadn't been able to make her feet move very fast.

When the assassin had stepped closer to Philip into the intersection, she'd frozen. Her only thought had been that she had to do something to save Philip, that she couldn't just stand helplessly by while he was murdered. Shooting the assassin in the arm had seemed like the logical choice.

The lantern Philip had brought with him into the tunnel sat where he'd abandoned it moments ago. The flame still flickered enough to see the hard line of his jaw and a new determination to survive.

A voice called out in Danish.

Yes, the man had to be another assassin. How many were there?

She crept closer to Philip and readied her revolver. Maybe if they shot at the man together, they'd be able to wound him enough that they could get away.

Philip replied in Danish, and the two went back and forth in a conversation for a minute or more.

Finally, Philip gently pushed her hand with the revolver down, lowering his at the same time. "He's been my bodyguard for the duration of my travels in your country."

"Do you believe him?"

"Yes. I've seen him at times and thought he was my assassin. But it turns out, he was keeping watch over me instead."

"What if he's just saying it?" She couldn't loosen her grip on the revolver, couldn't shake the fear that something bad still might happen to Philip.

"He believes the assassin finally tracked me to Fairplay the day of the storm, but he didn't show himself around town until yesterday, when the snow began to melt. Since the assassin couldn't get past the bodyguard, he figured out a way to manipulate me into doing what he asked."

"By kidnapping me?"

"Kidnapping the woman I love." Philip's voice turned husky with emotion as he pried the gun from her fingers.

She hadn't just imagined the words. He really had spoken them.

She wanted to throw herself into his arms and kiss him again, but she forced herself to stay where she was. She couldn't encourage Philip, had to make him leave as soon as possible. Even if this assassin was dead, there could be more—likely would be more.

"I was wrong to think we could be together." She spoke before she lost her courage. "You won't be safe in Fairplay any longer and need to go and hide in a new place."

He stuffed both of their guns in his belt, then took her hands in his. "Tonight, when I thought I would lose you, I realized that I never want to spend another day without you by my side."

Her body tensed with breathless need for him in return. She didn't want to think about not being with him tomorrow or the next day, much less for months on end. Maybe never. But if that was what it took to keep him out of harm's way, then she had to put aside her selfish needs. "The danger—"

He touched her lips with a finger. That was all it took for every thought to leave her head . . . except thoughts about his finger, which was now grazing her lip.

Oh, dear heavens. She couldn't let herself get carried away with her obsession with his touch. Not here. Not now.

His lips began to quirk up on one side, almost as if he knew the effect he had upon her. Almost as if he'd done it on purpose to silence her. She wanted to say something witty in return or touch him back, but her mind wouldn't work.

"We'll discuss our future later. For now, I want to return to town and let the doctor take a look at your wounds."

When he began to guide her toward the entrance, she didn't resist. The bodyguard had already disposed of the assassin's body. She didn't ask where, didn't want to know. All she cared about was that Philip was alive and well . . . and somehow, she had to keep him that way.

The bodyguard, a man by the name of Sven, brought Philip's horse around to the front entrance of the mine. He was quick to serve, respectful, and deferred to Philip in all things. He even bowed toward Philip on occasion. Philip accepted the special treatment, clearly accustomed to it.

Carrying a lantern, Sven led the way during the ride out of the narrow, overgrown gorge, down the mountain, and back into the foothills. Felicity sat in the saddle in front of Philip. With his arms surrounding her and his solid chest pressed against her, she could almost believe everything would be okay.

Since the medical clinic was closed, Philip took her straight to the doctor's mansion, set on the edge of town. Both doctors, Astrid and Logan, were home, and they tended to her wounds. When finished, Philip drove her wagon while she rode his horse out to the boardinghouse, with Sven leading the way once again.

Even though the chill and darkness of night had settled, Mrs. Keller and Serena rushed outside at the first sight of her, worried because she'd been gone so long without a word.

She started to explain all that had happened but then stopped abruptly and looked at Philip for guidance on how much to reveal. Even though she'd already forgiven him for deceiving her about his identity, she was beginning to understand why he'd done it. After just one day, she'd almost disclosed that he was a prince. How would she have kept his secret for weeks?

She let Philip tell the story about her kidnapping so that he could share as much or as little as he wanted about all that had transpired.

When the hour finally grew late, Philip insisted on staying at the boardinghouse for the night. She didn't protest. After everything that had happened, somehow the boardinghouse felt safer than town, even though that wasn't necessarily true.

Philip offered to watch Mr. Keller for the first shift of the night so that Mrs. Keller could sleep on the sofa. And as Philip situated himself beside the older man with a book in hand, Sven pulled up a chair in the kitchen and positioned it outside the bedroom door.

When Felicity finally crawled under her covers, she was too tired to keep her eyes open. She hugged her covers around her, gratitude swelling in her heart. Philip was safe and back at the boardinghouse where he belonged.

But was it where he belonged? And would she have the strength to send him on his way tomorrow as she knew she needed to?

23

Three days. Philip had sent the transatlantic telegram to the prime minister three days ago. And he hadn't heard back.

He'd been hoping for a return telegram from the prime minister and parliament with their thoughts about his plans. Although he wanted to respect the government and the law, he couldn't be bound so tightly in the matter of who he chose for his wife.

With or without their approval, he was moving forward. If someday Gustaf was no longer king and parliament rejected him for his decision, he was confident his younger sister Estelle could take the leadership, especially if he stood by her side and assisted her.

He paused in chopping wood to wipe perspiration from his forehead, the morning sunshine as beautiful as always in the high mountain country. Though the November air was crisp, the sky was as blue as a summer day.

He would miss this place with its wide openness and the rugged mountains surrounding it.

But today he was leaving. During a trip into town the previous afternoon with Sven, he'd learned the snow in the passes had finally melted enough for horses and riders to cross over. The way was wet and even slick in places, but the few travelers who'd made it up from Denver proved it was doable.

Yes, he was leaving today. And he was taking Felicity with him. She just didn't know it yet.

He drew in a breath, his nostrils filling with the scent of damp soil, the ground and grass still soggy from the melted snow. The air was also laden with the smell of freshly cut wood.

Sven had done most of the chopping, but Philip had wanted to do his part, too, in making sure the boardinghouse would be well taken care of over the winter. And now that the pile under the lean-to was double- and triple-stacked, there would be more than plenty.

He and Sven had also rebuilt the stalls in the barn, had stocked the loft with plenty of hay and feed for the livestock, and had even made repairs to the house in places where the storm had taken a toll.

Sven had made it clear that he didn't want Philip helping, always rushing to do everything for him and treating him like the royalty he was. Which was a big problem when they were still trying to keep his status as a prince undercover.

With how difficult it was for Sven to pretend a prince of Lapland was just an ordinary fellow, Philip better understood why the prime minister had instructed Sven not to interact with Philip at all but to remain anonymous.

As it was, even now Sven was gathering the pieces that Philip was chopping and adding them to the piles under the lean-to. The burly man was a constant presence at his side, and the lack of privacy and freedom had taken getting used to again, especially because it had allowed him no time alone with Felicity.

Strangely, neither the Kellers nor Serena had seemed perturbed by Sven's presence. They hadn't asked for an explanation for why the big fellow was there or where he'd come from. And if they thought Sven's behavior was strange, they didn't show it.

Sven held out his hand for the ax. "You're getting hot and sweaty. You can't have that today, can you?"

"You're right." Philip handed Sven the ax and took a step away from the chopping block. He dusted off his finest navy-blue trousers and then grabbed his matching blue coat from where he'd draped it over the lean-to railing.

Sven was at his side in the next instant, helping him don the coat. Philip bit back a sigh and a rebuke. Nothing he said could deter Sven from catering to his every whim.

As Sven lifted the coat and settled it on Philip's shoulders, Philip pulled the pocket watch from his vest and flipped open the case.

It was half past nine. Time to put into motion his carefully laid plans—the plans he'd spent yesterday afternoon initiating.

As though reading Philip's thoughts, Sven raised a brow. "Ready?" Sven spoke in English, reserving Danish for the times when he wanted to communicate privately.

Philip patted the inner pocket of his coat and nodded. "I'm ready." Even so, his pulse rushed forward with a mixture of anticipation and determination.

At the squeak of the front door, Philip started across the yard. Felicity was right on time.

As he neared the front porch, she was already descending in the purple gown she'd worn the afternoon that he'd taken her portrait and that he'd asked her to wear again today. Her hair, in all its fiery glory, was coiled into the chignon that showed off her neck, just the way he liked it.

He bounded the last few steps and offered her his arm gallantly. "My lady." He bowed with a flourish. "You look as ravishing as always."

Mrs. Keller and Serena with her little boy stood on the porch watching Felicity, pleased smiles upon their faces.

Although he wanted to wrap his arms around Felicity and kiss her into oblivion, he'd exerted incredible patience over the past few days. Just a little longer. That's what he'd been telling himself to hold back.

The wagon was waiting in front of the house, the old gelding hitched and ready to go. And of course, Sven had his horse saddled and intended to accompany them.

"Why won't you tell me where we're going?" Felicity asked as he led her toward the wagon, her hand tucked into the crook of his arm.

"It's a surprise, and by definition of a surprise, you aren't supposed to know."

"What if I don't want it to be a surprise?" Her brown eyes rounded with anticipation, and the slight curl of her lips hinted at just how much she was enjoying his scheming.

He patted his camera case and tripod as he passed by the back of the wagon. He'd already used the excuse that he wanted to get more photographs today, particularly one of them together. But he'd refrained from telling her the location of the pictures. And he didn't intend to tell her until they were there.

"I'll give you one clue. You get to spend the morning with an incredibly handsome man."

"I do?" She feigned innocence. "Then I'll look forward to meeting him."

He grinned and prayed he'd get a lifetime of such banter with her.

The trip to town was filled with more of her teasing questions. As they rolled down Main Street, his heart began to thud harder, and his palms grew damp. He could admit, he was a little nervous.

What if she didn't agree to his plans?

Over the past three days since the kidnapping, she'd been urging him to go someplace new and hide. She was afraid Gustaf had hired more than one assassin. But Sven had assured them he'd only ever seen the one. Sven had privately informed him that it wouldn't be long before Gustaf hired another, especially once he realized he was no longer receiving communication from his man.

That meant they had a blessed reprieve from the threat of death, and the urgency of leaving Fairplay had diminished.

Even so, Felicity was worried. Philip didn't blame her after what she'd experienced. But he'd asked her not to talk about their parting ways yet and instead to simply enjoy the extra few days they had together.

She'd agreed, but he'd still seen the hint of sadness in her eyes and had caught her looking at him with tears in her eyes on a couple of occasions, as though she was already bracing herself for his departure.

Except that he'd meant his resolve. He didn't intend to part ways with her . . . ever.

As the wagon rolled to a stop, Felicity glanced around. "We're getting our pictures taken in town?"

"Is there something wrong with that?"

She peered around at the boardwalks caked with dried mud, the rutted street still filled with puddles, and the gray, weathered buildings with their false fronts. Fairplay itself wasn't a beautiful or picturesque town, but with the mountains in the distance on every side, he'd grown attached to the place. Or maybe he liked the town because of the woman he'd met there.

Whatever the case, he helped her down from the wagon, then strolled alongside her down the boardwalk with Sven only a few paces behind.

"Are you ready for the greatest day of your life?" He tried to tame the flock of birds attempting to take flight inside him.

She quirked a brow. "Greatest day?"

"It will be the greatest day for me, if you say yes." He stopped.

"And what exactly am I saying yes to?"

He opened the door that was next to them. The church door. "Say yes to marrying me."

24

Marry Philip?

Felicity drew in a sharp breath.

Was Philip proposing?

As if hearing her unasked question, in the next instant, he was lowering himself to his knee in front of her, still holding one of her hands. He peered up at her, his smile growing and his eyes crinkling at the corners. "I want to marry you, Felicity. And I want you to come with me wherever I go and be with me always."

With her free hand, she pinched herself. Was this a dream?

At a movement behind them inside the church, she sucked in another breath. Charity and Patience and their husbands were beaming at her near the altar. In front of them stood Father Zieber, his prayer book open, the candelabras lit, and a smile upon his face.

After three months apart from Charity, Felicity

wanted to rush into the church and give her sister a hug. A dozen questions also clamored for answers. Topmost among them was why Charity was back in Fairplay and when had she arrived.

But with Philip on his knee in front of her, his handsome face filled with expectation and his blue eyes brimming with love, she cast aside the questions and focused on the man she loved.

"Please say yes to marrying me," he said again, "and make me the happiest man on earth."

The word *yes* pushed for release, but she bit it back. He was a prince, and he'd already once told her that he didn't have the freedom to choose his own wife without the input of his government. But she couldn't very well say that here. Not with everyone looking on.

"I thought you couldn't," she whispered. "What about the law?"

"I don't care," he whispered in return. "I sent a telegram. I asked for their support but told them I intended to marry the woman I love regardless."

"What if they decide to punish you for it?" She wasn't sure how a government could punish a prince. Would they take away his title? Ban him from the country? Force him into exile?

"I am still willing to do my duty if the day should come that they want me to become—" Still on his knees, he cast a sideways glance toward their onlookers in the church.

She knew he was referring to the kingship if Gustaf was deposed. They'd talked about it more over the past few days together, and Philip had explained all that had transpired with Gustaf, the populace's dissatisfaction, and the growing turmoil. He'd also told her about the laws and regulations and the elected governing body, all of which Gustaf had ignored as he'd taken control of the country.

After their conversations, she wholeheartedly supported Philip's need to take the kingship and serve his country. "I don't want to be the cause of you not fulfilling your destiny."

"You won't be." He dropped his voice again so that no one could hear their conversation. "I assured the prime minister I shall still be my country's humble servant in any capacity but shall do so with you by my side."

"And what was the reply?"

"He hasn't responded." He lifted her hand to his lips and placed a gentle kiss there.

Although the touch was light, the tenderness, the adoration, and the desire promised much more to come—a promise that she wasn't sure she was ready to accept. Not because she didn't want all he was offering but because she loved him too much to hold him back from his future.

"I want to marry you here today. Now." His voice was raspy with wanting. "Because I can't bear the thought of spending a single second more of my life away from you."

She couldn't imagine it either, but she had to be sure he knew the consequences of such a decision, that he might forfeit becoming Lapland's next king because of her. He'd already told her he'd never wished to be king, never planned on it, and never sought after it. But he'd also explained how he'd always known it was a possibility that he would take the throne if something ever happened to Gustaf. He'd just never expected the country would fight to take the kingship from Gustaf in order to give it to him.

"Are you sure you want to risk so much for me?"

"I've never been more certain about anything. Someone wise once told me that if the future is so uncertain, then we should make the most of every day we have left. And that's what I want to do."

"Someone wise? Or someone *very, very* wise?"

The blue of his eyes brightened with mirth. "Someone not only very, very wise but also very, very beautiful."

"Then I suppose we really must do as she suggested."

"I agree."

She could feel the worry from the past few days slipping slowly away. She was under no illusion the future would be easy. It would likely be full of hardships, especially if Gustaf sent another assassin after Philip. And if she was ever able to travel to Lapland with Philip, life in a new land with new customs would be difficult. She'd have much to learn and many adjustments.

But if Philip could learn all he had over the past year of his traveling, surely she could rise to the challenge and do the same.

He brushed his thumb across her ring finger. "So, will you make this the greatest day of my life by marrying me?"

"First you have to do one thing." She tugged at him to bring him up.

"One thing?" His voice turned low and seductive as he rose. "What exactly do you have in mind?" His attention fixed upon her lips.

"What do you think it is?"

"I know what I'm hoping it is."

"You might be right." She tipped her face up, giving him access to her.

At the same time, he bent and lightly brushed his nose against hers. "Should I give it a try and see if I am?"

"You may as well." With each teasing quip, her heart was growing lighter.

As he gently plied at her lips, the kiss captivated her, as each of his touches did. And hundreds of sensations swirled through her so that she was afraid that if she breathed, she'd release a groan instead.

She wanted to languidly devour his mouth in return, but with everyone looking on, she dragged in a deep inhale of him, then forced herself to release the kiss.

His mouth hovered near hers, his breathing shallow and heated and filled with need. "Ready?" His voice was rumbly as he ran his hand down her arm and wrapped his fingers through hers.

She was definitely ready, but she couldn't get the word out past her breathlessness. Instead, she nodded and took her place at his side. Then she stepped into the small church and allowed him to lead her down the aisle to become his bride.

Charity and Patience stood beside their handsome husbands, and they were radiating happiness, both of them more beautiful than she'd remembered. Was that what the love of a good man could do? Make a woman flourish so that she became even more beautiful?

She didn't know how Philip had been able to make all the arrangements for the wedding and find a way for her sisters to both be there—especially Charity—but her heart swelled with gladness that they could be present to witness her pledging her life to the man she loved.

"Thank you," she whispered to him as they reached the front. "For arranging all this."

"You're welcome." He cocked his head, a gleam in his eyes—one that told her he'd loved surprising her and that he'd relish doing so again and again.

She cocked her head in return and hoped he could read the expression in her eyes—one that said she'd never tire of it.

Wherever life might take them next, this was where she wanted to be—by his side holding his hand. She prayed that she would have a lifetime to do so. And a lifetime to show him just how much he'd captivated her, body, soul, and spirit.

25

"I now pronounce that they be man and wife together. In the name of the Father, of the Son, and of the Holy Ghost. Amen."

As Father Zieber spoke the last words of the ceremony, Philip's heart welled with both relief and joy. The ring he'd purchased and had in his coat pocket was now on Felicity's finger, the ceremony was complete, and they'd had witnesses to their union in the sight of God and man, including Sven. Nothing could separate them now.

As Felicity peered up at him, her cheeks were flushed and her eyes alight. And her lips were so soft and pliable that he ached with the need to kiss her again.

Father Zieber took a step back and closed his prayer book. Then he smiled. "I can see that you'd like to kiss your bride, Philip."

"Guess I've never been good at being subtle."

The guests laughed lightly, and Felicity only flushed all the more.

He wasn't ashamed of how much he wanted her. In fact, he intended to revel in how much he wanted her and make sure she knew it every single day.

He lowered his head. This time, he planned to lose himself in their kiss, and he didn't care who was watching. But as his lips tasted the sweet corner of hers, the back door of the church banged open with enough force to shake the walls.

Sven was already charging toward the door, his revolver out and aimed at the intruder.

Captain Jim hunched in the doorway, hopped back, and lifted both hands in the air, his eyes widening. "I didn't do it. I swear!"

Sven lowered his revolver and stuffed it back into his holster before pretending to straighten his shirt and coat as though he hadn't just held someone at gunpoint.

Captain Jim held out two folded slips of paper. "These just came in at the post office. Reckon since Philip—Mr. Berg's—been waiting on them, I thought I'd deliver them on my way back to the store."

Sven, already halfway down the aisle, finished crossing toward Captain Jim. With a glare, he snatched up the telegrams almost as if the poor store owner had committed a crime by holding them.

Captain Jim raised his hand, clearly intimidated by

Sven—another reason why the prime minister had been wise to have Sven stay as covert as possible over the past year. The burly man was about as subtle as a moose at a tea party.

Sven walked both telegrams over to Philip, not taking the slightest peek at them. He wouldn't. His sense of honor was too strong.

Captain Jim didn't move from his spot in the doorway, was watching Philip with a strange quirk to his brow.

As Philip took the telegrams, Sven met his gaze evenly, knowing all that was at stake. He gave a nod, one of encouragement.

Even so, Philip's stomach clenched. Old insecurities welled up to wage war inside, especially the need to please everyone. Although there was value in compromise and listening to all sides on a matter, his marriage to Felicity was final. He'd never change it, not from any amount of pressure.

Hesitating but a moment more, he unfolded the first telegram. The message was short and simple: *Sven's investigation of new wife received. Majority has voted to accept her.*

Sven's investigation?

The bodyguard's granite expression didn't change, not even a twitch. Now wasn't the time or place to question the man, but clearly he'd been in more communication with the prime minister than he'd let on.

"What did they say?" Felicity asked breathlessly.

"They've accepted you." The relief at their decision hit Philip the moment he spoke the words. Yes, he'd been willing to defy his government and the laws, but he could admit that, deep inside, he'd wanted them to accept Felicity and see what a beautiful and special person she was the same way he had.

She launched against him and hugged him tightly. His arms wrapped around her in response, and he breathed her in. Somehow she'd become the air he needed. Without her, he'd wither and die.

"Your Royal Majesty," Sven said. "You really should read the second telegram."

At the formal title of address, Felicity's sisters and brothers-in-law began to whisper among themselves. Father Zieber's brows rose above confused eyes. And Captain Jim watched the whole interaction with curiosity. Had the older man already read the telegram? Was he waiting for an explanation?

Sven's words finally penetrated. He hadn't said *Royal Highness*. He'd said *Royal Majesty*.

Before Philip could protest, the bodyguard lowered to one knee, bowed his head, and said in a booming voice, "Long live King Carl Philip!"

The murmuring around him turned into questions and confusion.

With pounding heart, Philip opened the second telegram. It was as simple and yet as profound as the first: *Gustaf is dead. Long live King Carl Philip.*

In the next moment, Sven shifted and bowed toward Felicity. "Long live Queen Felicity."

Felicity cupped a hand over her mouth to capture a gasp. But her eyes met Philip's, full of questions.

He nodded.

She wavered, grabbed on to the nearest pew. And in the next instant, Sven was gently helping her sit down. Her sisters crowded around, hugging her and bombarding her with a thousand questions. And he was left to face their husbands, Hudson and Spencer.

Thankfully the two men didn't seem to make much ado about his royal status. He answered their queries as best he could, still reeling from the knowledge that in an instant, he'd gone from prince to king of his country.

The deep love of his country and desire to rule it well swelled within him, and he was suddenly anxious to return and begin the hard work of healing a fractured nation.

As Felicity hugged with her sisters again, she finally turned to him, holding back, her expression guarded. "What do you think of everything?"

"I think I'm ready to go home." It was the truth, and he couldn't deny it.

Sven nodded, his expression pleased but solemn.

"Your Majesty, the prime minister wants you to return with all haste."

Felicity hugged her arms over her chest as if to ward off a chill. "The boardinghouse needs someone to manage it—"

"Hudson and I will take care of everything." Charity, who had the same red hair as Felicity, spoke reassuringly. "We'd already made the decision to return early. In fact, we'd traveled as far as Denver when the snowstorm hit."

Charity, now tucked against her husband, smiled up at him. Hudson didn't smile in return, but his eyes softened and filled with adoration. The fellow was clearly madly in love with his wife.

Charity turned her gaze back on Felicity. "When Philip somehow managed to track us down and telegram us two days ago about the wedding plans, we knew we had to find a way to make it over Kenosha Pass, and we did. When we met Philip yesterday evening, we gave him our full support."

Upon receiving the telegram about the plans to marry Felicity, Hudson had launched an investigation. Apparently the fellow's money could get him whatever information he desired, and he'd been able to uncover Philip's true identity. Thankfully, Hudson and Charity had kept their discovery private.

Felicity studied her sister's face. "But I don't know if I'll fit in—"

"If anyone can rise to the challenge, it's you." Patience, who was soft-spoken but equally beautiful with her blond hair and blue eyes, squeezed Felicity's arm and smiled gently at her. Patience's husband had his arm around her too, as if he couldn't quite get his fill of her.

Philip had the feeling he was going to like his new brothers-in-law. At the very least he could empathize with how besotted they each were with their wives. Because he felt the same way with Felicity.

Patience kissed Felicity's cheek. "You go and live your life and have those adventures you've always dreamed about."

Felicity nodded, but doubts flitted across her delicate features. Was she already regretting her decision to marry him?

Philip bent and scooped her up into his arms, holding her captive against him, determined to carry her back to Lapland if he had to.

Her eyes rounded. "What are you doing?"

"I am taking captive what's mine."

Even as she began to shake her head in protest, her arms wrapped around his neck. "You can't take me. I'm not good enough to be queen—"

He cut off her doubts the best way he knew how. He covered her mouth, ravishing her lips and showing her exactly how *good enough* she was for him. He may have *taken* her captive, but she had captivated him totally and completely. He was hers. Always.

Only Father Zieber's throat-clearing and the guffaws of his brothers-in-law kept him from losing himself in the kiss.

As he pulled back just slightly, her breath and heat and skin tempted him to keep going, but he forced himself to speak as earnestly as he could. "I'm not good enough to be king, but that won't stop me from doing the very best I can. That's all anyone will expect of me. And that's all they'll expect of you."

Although her cheeks were flushed, her eyes radiated earnestness. "Are you sure?"

"I am very sure." He tenderly traced her jawline with his knuckles. "I, on the other hand, will have many expectations of you."

Her lips lifted in the beginning of a smile. "Not as many as I will have of you."

A thrill rushed through him. "Name one."

Her fingers at the back of his neck sank into his hair and drew his head down to hers. "You must kiss me as frequently as possible."

"I think I can do that, especially since that was one of my expectations of you."

Her lips grazing his widened into a full smile. "Then prove it."

And he did.

AUTHOR'S NOTE

Thank you, Readers, for taking another trip to the Colorado high country with my Colorado Cowgirl series and *Captivated by the Cowgirl*. I hope you enjoyed the secret royal storyline just as much as I enjoyed writing it. I always love reading about royalty and decided to have a prince (of a totally made up country!) make an appearance this time.

Again, I want to take a second to thank the many people who made this series (and this book) possible. Dear Rel, what would I do without you?! You're not only my assistant but also my friend, and I'm eternally grateful for you.

Many, many thanks to Roseanna White my cover designer, especially on this cover. Thank you for putting up with our delays as we finagled over getting the perfect image! Also, many, many thanks to my editor Katie Donovan for polishing my books into true gems.

Thank you to all my beta readers who are on my First

Readers team! I am supremely thankful for your keen eyes in catching all those last lingering typos. Many hugs and much thanks to Zanese, Edward, Carrie, Stacey, and Jessica for helping me with this fourth book in the series.

Finally, thank you, Readers, for all your support and encouragement! Be on the lookout for Weston's story, which is coming soon! After his heartache, he deserves a happily ever after, don't you think? You'll get to meet his big family and all his siblings (who, as it turns out, are demanding that their stories be told, so watch for a new western series in 2024!).

To stay up to date on all my books, visit my website at jodyhedlund.com. Or join my Facebook Reader Room at facebook.com/groups/jodyhedlundsreaderroom.

Jody Hedlund is the bestselling author of more than forty novels and is the winner of numerous awards. Jody lives in Michigan with her husband, busy family, and five spoiled cats. She writes sweet historical romances with plenty of sizzle.

A complete list of my novels can be found at jodyhedlund.com.

Would you like to know when my next book is available? You can sign up for my newsletter, become my friend on Goodreads, like me on Facebook, or follow me on Twitter.

Newsletter: jodyhedlund.com

Facebook: AuthorJodyHedlund

Twitter: @JodyHedlund

The more reviews a book has, the more likely other readers are to find it. If you have a minute, please leave a rating or review. I appreciate all reviews, whether positive or negative.

Printed in the USA
CPSIA information can be obtained
at www.ICGtesting.com
LVHW041735070524
779549LV00003B/418